"I need to go on working with the kids," said Megan. "Can't I practice with the team part of the time and race on weekends? I'm sure that one of the Tadpole parents could run the Sunday races."

Jeff looked at her angrily. "You expect me to sell that idea to the team? I just told you they resent all your missed practices."

Megan looked down at her hands. "Well, it looks like either I give up the kids or I give up the team. Is that it?"

Jeff stopped and turned. "I guess that's it. If you decide that the coaching job is all that important, I don't think there's much left of our relationship."

"I suppose I know how you feel," Megan whispered.

"I don't understand why you're even considering leaving the Dolphins—and splitting us up. We need you, Megan. *I* need you." Then Jeff pulled her into his arms for a long, tender kiss that left her feeling weak and uncertain.

Bantam Sweet Dreams Romances
Ask your bookseller for the books you have missed

# Summer Breezes

### Susan Blake

BANTAM BOOKS
TORONTO · NEW YORK · LONDON · SYDNEY

RL 6, IL age 11 and up

SUMMER BREEZES
*A Bantam Book / April 1984*

*Sweet Dreams and its associated logo are registered trademarks of
Bantam Books, Inc. Registered in U.S. Patent and Trademark Office
and elsewhere.*

*Cover photo by Pat Hill.*

ISBN 0-553-24097-8

*Published simultaneously in the United States and Canada*

---

Bantam Books are published by Bantam Books, Inc. Its trademark,
consisting of the words ''Bantam Books'' and the portrayal of a
rooster, is Registered in U.S. Patent and Trademark Office and in
other countries. Marca Registrada. Bantam Books, Inc., 666 Fifth
Avenue, New York, New York 10103.

---

PRINTED IN THE UNITED STATES OF AMERICA

O     0 9 8 7 6 5 4 3 2 1

*For Robin and Amy—my two favorite girls*

# Chapter One

The late-afternoon June light cast long shadows as Megan Woods and Carole Tyler checked the last mooring line at the end of the boat dock. To the west, against the glowing sky, a dark mass of thunderclouds was rising. Megan made a careful final inspection of the dinghy rack to be sure the masts and rudders they had taken off the boats were stored so they wouldn't shift around. A storm was blowing up, and she didn't want the Tadpoles' new coach to come on Saturday to find the boat dock littered with the equipment they had forgotten to tie down or stow away.

With the back of her hand, Megan pushed a damp wisp of blond hair out of her eyes.

1

"Looks like we've taken care of everything," she said.

The dozen boats that belonged to the Tadpoles were stacked neatly three by three in the red-painted rack; the sails were folded and placed in the wooden lockers; and the entire area had been policed with great care and lots of noise.

"The kids did a pretty good job of everything," Carole replied, glancing around. "They get better about cleanup all the time." She paused thoughtfully and began coiling a short length of line. "So, I guess this is the last time we'll be doing this together."

Megan bent down and began packing her gear bag. *Why do good things always have to come to an end?* she thought unhappily. She had helped Carole coach the Tadpoles for the last two months only, but that had been long enough for her to get really close to the fifteen kids in the group. Now it was all over because Carole had found a new job and was moving to Houston.

Oh, well, in a few days the commodore would announce the new coach, and Megan could look forward to a summer of full-time sailing with the Dolphins, the yacht club's senior racing team. She wouldn't have to miss any more practices or races now that her time wouldn't be committed to the Tadpoles.

Megan frowned. She'd also be working for her mother, helping her with her catering service, and she definitely *wasn't* enthusiastic about that. Still, she knew her mother had worked hard to keep things going for the two of them since the divorce, and it wasn't fair to be embarrassed by what she'd chosen to do for a living. It was just that none of the Dolphins' mothers had to work, much less run a catering service. That was almost like working in somebody's kitchen, for heaven's sake. Even though none of the Dolphins had mentioned it to her—her boyfriend, Jeff Freeman, even seemed to enjoy hearing her mother tell funny stories about some of her clients— she knew they thought it was strange. They probably talked about it when she wasn't around. She sighed. Why couldn't her mother have chosen something else to do, something a little more ordinary.

"You know, Megan," Carole said, interrupting her thoughts, "you're really a terrific sailing teacher. Of course you know all about handling a boat, setting a course, predicting wind shifts, and all that stuff. But best of all, you can communicate what you know without confusing the kids. So many good sailors are terrible teachers, especially for youngsters. All you need is a little more confidence in yourself, and you'll be a great teacher."

Megan felt a warm glow of pleasure at Carole's words, but it faded quickly against the chilly recollection that that day was the last she'd be helping with the Tadpoles. Dejected, she sat down on the overturned hull of one of the dinghies and wrapped her arms around her knees. "I'm going to miss you, Carole," she said glumly, trying to swallow the regret that stuck in her throat. "I've learned so many things these last two months, about sailing and about kids, too. All I used to want to do was sail for myself. But now I've learned that it's more fun, really, to help others. Especially these kids."

"I know just what you mean, Megan, though most people probably think we're a little strange for feeling that way."

*That's for sure*, Megan thought. The Dolphins definitely didn't understand. All they cared about was sailing, racing, partying, and having fun. Of course, that was one of the things that had attracted her to the Dolphins in the first place. When Megan and her mother had moved to Texas after the divorce, she'd been drawn to the Dolphins as a group of self-assured, sophisticated kids. She wanted more than anything to belong. And since she and Jeff had started dating, nearly six months before, they'd really seemed to accept her and include her in their fun.

But things had changed for Megan now. She still loved winning races with the Dolphins. She still loved partying and sailing out to Surprise Island for the nighttime picnics with the gang. But she didn't want to give up the Tadpoles. She just loved teaching the kids to sail. Megan swallowed hard and tried to smile. "Do you know yet who's going to be the new coach?" she asked. Her voice sounded strained.

"Nope, haven't heard a word," Carole said, tossing the neatly coiled line into a blue locker. She glanced at her watch. "Hey, it's after seven, and I need to catch the commodore before the regatta committee meeting. And if you don't hurry, you're going to miss your picnic. Jeff must be wondering what's keeping you."

Megan looked up the hill toward the clubhouse. She could see smoke curling lazily from the barbecue on the clubhouse patio. They must have begun the picnic already.

5

"Oh, my gosh!" she exclaimed. "I didn't think it was so late! Jeff's going to kill me."

"Well, come on, kid, pack it in and get crackin'." Carole gave her a playful shove. "I'll finish up here."

Megan threw her arms around Carole. "Oh, I'll miss you and the Tadpoles," she cried. Then she quickly slung her red canvas gear bag over her shoulder and jogged up the stairs that angled steeply up the hill to the club-house. She paused at the top to look out over Cedar Lake, admiring, as she always did, the serenity of the water surrounded by green hills and bare, weathered limestone bluffs. She had lived in Texas for almost a year, since the beginning of her junior year, and she had finally come to feel at home with the slower, more relaxed pace of Texas living. It was different from the hectic, fast pace of the Detroit suburb where she and her parents had lived until the divorce. The vast expanses of rolling grasslands, dotted with clumps of lacy mesquite trees and gray-brown cedar, always took her breath away. To the west, she knew, millions of acres of Texas were flat and dry and dusty, without a single tree, but the land around Cedar Springs was lush and green with many clear streams that tumbled noisily through the woods. It wasn't at all like the barren, sagebrush-covered Texas she'd imagined in Detroit after seeing a few Westerns.

Directly below she could see the protected inlet where dozens of sailboats were moored in neat rows. Close to the mouth of the cove was the Tadpoles' dock, the dinghies stacked tidily in their racks. Farther away from the clubhouse stairs and at the back of the inlet was the small dock where the Dolphins moored their five white Fireballs. Megan could just glimpse the silver mast and white hull of *Windhover*, Mindy Harris's boat, which the two of them would be racing in for the summer. We really are a good team, she thought with a surge of pride, good enough to have a real chance to win the Cedar Lake Cup at the end of the summer season.

But as much as she enjoyed sailing with Mindy, Megan had to admit that she liked taking the boat out by herself even more. She loved to sail, the boat tilting sharply as she leaned against the wind, using her body for balance. It was almost comforting to feel her ankles snugged tight under the hiking straps, her fingers light and steady on the tiller. Sailing made her feel in control; she could choose a goal and a direction and achieve it, even when the wind wasn't working for her or when it challenged her strength and endurance.

She sighed. It was too bad she didn't feel the same control and self-confidence all the time. On the boat she instinctively knew where she was and where she wanted to go—and even the quickest way to get there. But the rest of her life was spent drifting along with a current she didn't have any control over, feeling uncertain and indecisive.

"Hey, Megan, get a move on!" Mindy was standing beside the grill, waving a hot dog speared on a fork. Gary Burns and Mark Donnelly were standing beside her, helping themselves to more buns. "We're having seconds," Gary called, "and Jeff is going to take care of yours if you don't hurry."

Megan could smell the hot dogs cooking, and she wrinkled her nose hungrily, abandoning the view of the lake and her troublesome thoughts. "Don't burn mine," she called and broke into a lope. "I'm starved!"

# Chapter Two

"Well, slowpoke, what in the world kept you so long?"

Jeff was sitting with Mark and Louise Stern at a picnic table, balancing an empty plastic plate on a soft-drink can and looking bored and more than a little irritated. There were three or four others at the table, too, plates piled with hot dogs and potato salad. Several kids glanced at her curiously as she dashed up, and one or two wigwagged a casual hello, but their reception wasn't particularly enthusiastic.

Even when he was scowling, as he was then, Jeff was still the best-looking boy Megan had ever met. He was close to six feet tall, sun-browned, with a permanent peeling patch across his nose, and blond hair bleached almost white by the summer sun. He was the Dolphins' senior skipper—and the most popular boy at Cedar Springs High. He had asked her out for the first time just after she and Mindy had won the Frostbite Series the past December. Since then, Jeff and Megan's relationship had grown more and more comfortable, fed by the sharing of racing and sailing.

All spring—until Megan had started working with the Tadpoles, that is—they'd spent every spare moment together. Most of the time, Megan had to admit, they were either sailing or getting ready to go sailing or *talking* about sailing. And sometimes she wished they could go off by themselves, away from the ever-present Dolphins. Still, Megan was happy to be popular as were all the Dolphins, and especially happy to be going with Jeff.

But sometimes, and especially recently, Megan felt a nagging uncertainty about Jeff, who had a lot of friends, many of them girls, most of these pretty and sophisticated. And in her darker moments Megan couldn't imagine why in the world he found her interesting. She was only *middling*, she thought despairingly at these times. Hair a middling blond, not shiny ash blond, like Mindy's, but dark blond and streaked by the sun. It was cut in a wedge that Megan liked because it stayed pretty neat all by itself. Middling gray eyes with heavy dark lashes, wide spaced in a face that had no special features except for the few freckles that were dusted across a small, turned-up nose. Nothing about her stood out, she thought, nothing except the fact that she dated Jeff Freeman and was a member of the Dolphin Sailing Team.

Of course, the basic problem, she reminded herself glumly from time to time, was that this kind of specialness was only superficial. It was sort of like wearing a princess costume for Halloween or playing the lead in the senior play, she thought. Sooner or later somebody was bound to discover that the *real* you wasn't a princess or a leading lady. The *real* you was just a very, very ordinary person.

But Megan was also troubled by the Dolphins' recent attitude toward her—it seemed to have changed. Before, they had always enjoyed having her as a part of the group. But now they—well, they seemed to resent the time she spent with the Tadpoles. In one way, Megan could understand why;

11

she had had to miss a couple of races because of the Tadpoles. And Jeff had given her permission to miss some of the practice sessions, too. But surely *that* couldn't make any difference in the way the group felt about her, could it? These were her closest friends—her only friends.

But the worst part wasn't the change in the Dolphins, it was the gradual change in Jeff. In the last two months they hadn't seen each other quite so often. Megan was often busy with the Tadpoles, and Jeff spent all of his spare time working out with the Dolphins. And when they did get together, Jeff seemed quiet and distant. It was hard to talk with him about the Tadpoles because she knew he'd rather have her working with the Dolphins. Their conversations were awkward, stiff, and stilted. That night, Megan thought, looked as if it were going to be one of the more difficult nights.

Jeff unfolded his bare tanned legs and turned to look at Megan. He was wearing a white open-necked short-sleeved shirt and a pair of crisp white sailing shorts that made Megan feel grubby in her faded red T-shirt and worn denim cut-offs. If only she'd taken a few extra minutes to clean up, at least comb her hair and put on some mascara.

"Mindy was getting ready to serve your hot dogs to the fish," he said quietly. There was a note of annoyance in his husky voice. "We thought maybe you'd decided to spend the evening with the Tadpoles. Or maybe you just forgot about us?"

"Of course I didn't forget," she said. "Carole and I decided to run capsize drills this afternoon, and we had our hands full." She dumped her gear bag on the grass and plopped down next to it to search for her comb. She was disappointed by Jeff's impatience, but she was angry at herself, too, for being late.

Mindy set a red plastic plate at Megan's place, heaped with two hot dogs, a double spoonful of spicy ranch beans, and a huge mound of potato salad. "Well, we're glad you're here, late or not." Mindy's shorts were also sparkling white, and she was wearing a red-and-white print blouse tied halter-style, with a matching red clip in her hair. "I wouldn't let any of these guys touch yours, even when they tried to steal it off the grill." She smiled brightly at Megan. "Anyway, this is a celebration—your last day with the little kids, right? Now you and I can get to work on our racing."

Mark came around the table carrying a cooler full of icy cold soft-drink cans. "I'll say all right to that," he drawled loudly, a biting edge in his voice. He dropped the cooler with a crash. "You two are our big winners. We can't afford to let either of you get lazy. We need your points."

"And don't forget," Louise said grimly, dishing another spoonful of potato salad onto her plate, "we're down a dozen points from last year just because you missed the last three races."

Kneeling on the ground, Megan looked up, startled by the anger in Louise's voice. She wished she could toss off a light, witty comment, but she couldn't think of anything to say, and the silence stretched out painfully until Mindy interrupted it.

"So all right already," she said, with just the right touch of humor. "Megan and I appreciate your supreme confidence that the two of us can keep all the rest of you afloat—so to speak." She turned to Jeff. "Anyway, now that we're up to full strength again, it won't take us long to get going. Right, Jeff?"

Jeff relaxed and swung his right leg over

14

the picnic-table seat, straddling it. "Mindy's right," he said with authority, glancing in Megan's direction. "Let's not jump all over Megan just because she had to spend time with the Tadpole toddlers."

Megan winced at his patronizing tone, but Mindy smothered a giggle, and Jeff looked pleased. "We all know that she only did it because the commodore asked her to. And because she wanted to help the yacht club until the new coach had been hired. But she's back now." He leaned over, put a firm hand on Megan's wrist, and looked intently into her eyes. "And we're not letting her go. She's too valuable. Now let her eat so we can get to the committee meeting on time."

He let go with a quick, light squeeze, and Megan stood up and took her seat wordlessly. It was all over now, all settled. Her job with the Tadpoles was over. The Dolphins still wanted her, still needed her, were still her friends—some of them, at least. And Jeff really didn't mean to be snobby about the kids. He just wanted the best for the Dolphins. She smiled as Mindy handed her a cold soda. "Thanks," she said gratefully.

"There's no need for thanks, we just have to score lots of points in all the races," Mindy

15

answered flatly. "Jeff's right. We've got to practice like crazy if we're going to win the Cedar Lake Cup."

"Hey, Jeff, have we got all the details ironed out for our part of the Firecracker Regatta?" Gary inquired, opening another ginger ale and downing half of it. "The commodore's going to ask us for a report at the meeting tonight."

"Yep, everything's under control," Jeff said. "Louise is lining up the trophies, and Joe's handling publicity. Looks like we're in pretty good shape." He popped a brownie into his mouth and chewed thoughtfully. "Except we still have some space problems, just like last year. Unless we can find more dock space, we'll have to turn away some of the small-boat entrants. Anybody got any ideas on that one?" Nobody answered, and Jeff went on. "Anyway, the regatta's only five weeks away, and the commodore's probably got a long list of chores for us, in addition to being in charge of small boats."

"You'd better believe it," Roger remarked in a deep, raspy voice. He was a chubby, round-faced boy who had been Megan's lab partner—not a very good one—in chemistry. "At last year's Firecracker, the commodore put me in charge of the Watermelon Derby. I had to go out and buy twenty watermelons and lug them here in the backseat of my dad's Jeep. I must have hauled watermelons for two hours, and then it rained, and we had to call the derby off."

Joe laughed shortly. "Yeah, I know all about dirty work. Louise and I drew grounds detail, and we were out here until almost midnight cleaning up after everyone left. The only thing the commodore wants out of us is *work*."

"But that's just not true," Megan said impulsively. Suddenly everyone was silent, looking at her, and she gulped in embarrassment. "That is—well, I mean, the commodore said that he wanted us to get involved in all the details so we'd learn how to run a regatta. And I have the feeling that he thinks we're too interested in our own stuff, that our interests are too limited." She looked down at her plate, her cheeks flaming. Why in the world had she said that? It sounded as though she were against all of them.

The silence stretched out. Finally Gary stood up and began to gather up the dishes. "Come on, gang, if we don't lay off the funny stories and get our act in gear, they'll kick us off the committee before we have a chance to get our assignments."

As they began to clean up the picnic table and pack away the leftovers, Megan avoided Jeff's eyes. She knew she hadn't gotten the evening off to a very good start. And when he came over and laid his arm over her shoulders, she looked up at him, surprised. He bent down, closer.

"Hey, don't take our teasing so seriously," he whispered in her ear. "Everybody likes you more than you think."

Megan laughed, not very convincingly. "Well, better tell that to Louise and Mark," she whispered back, trying to appear unconcerned but not doing a very good job. "I don't think they're exactly thrilled to see me."

But Jeff's tender words had made the evening seem brand-new again, and Megan started her part of the clean-up chores with a lighter heart.

# Chapter Three

"Hey, Megan, wait up!"

Halfway up the path from the picnic area to the stone-and-timber clubhouse, Megan paused and turned. It was Mindy, running up the hill with Louise in tow. "Louise wanted to tell you something," she said breathlessly when they had caught up.

With an I-wish-I-weren't-here look, Louise said in a rush, "I—I just wanted to say that I hope I didn't hurt your feelings or anything tonight. It's just that—well, we want to win the Summer Series, and you've been missing a lot of practices since you started working with the Tadpoles, and we all thought—"

Megan was speechless with surprise.

She'd never heard Louise apologize for anything. But she didn't have a chance to respond because Mindy broke in. "OK, Louise, that's good enough," she said, making a comic face.

Louise grinned. "Guess that last bit sounded pretty tacky, didn't it? Anyway, we're glad to have you back on board." Without waiting for a reply, she turned and jogged up the hill, her hair bouncing as she went.

Megan stared after her in amazement. She and Louise had never been what you'd call good friends. Mindy had said once that Louise was probably too competitive to be friends with anybody—she always wanted to beat everybody else. And that spirit of competition probably explained her reaction that night. Louise was convinced that the Dolphins had lost the Spring Series because Megan missed some races, and more than anything else in the world, she wanted to win.

But why had she changed her mind? After her angry words at the picnic, Megan might have expected almost anything from her, anything except an apology, fumbling as it was.

"Did you put Louise up to that?" she asked quietly.

Mindy scuffed her white sneakers against a rock, her face screened by her flowing blond hair. "No, I didn't have anything to do with it," she said. "But I think you ought to know who did."

"What do you mean?"

Mindy turned toward her. "It was Jeff. He said that Louise and Mark and some of the others were coming down too hard on you and that we needed to cooperate, not blame you. He kind of chewed us out."

Megan sighed. All her doubts about Jeff's feelings for her suddenly evaporated. He'd stood up for her in front of all his friends! "Jeff made Louise apologize?" she whispered.

Mindy laughed shortly, tossing her hair away from her face. "Well, he's the skipper, isn't he? It's his job to build cooperation." She paused and added thoughtfully, "Anyway, he's right. We've got a new series and a whole new season ahead of us. We ought to stop arguing and start working together." She looked squarely and seriously at Megan. "But Jeff means you, too, when he says that we all have to work together. Everybody on the team knows that you've had some special favors lately because Jeff happens to be your boy-friend."

Megan's mouth went dry. "Special favors?"

"If any of us missed as many races as you have, we'd be off the team so fast you couldn't even wave goodbye," Mindy said bluntly, her eyes flashing. "And some of the kids are a little resentful. They think Jeff ought to let somebody else try out for your place so we'd be sure to have somebody for every single race, not just when it suits her schedule."

Megan felt as though Mindy had slapped her. For the first time, she could see clearly how the others looked at it. She understood why the Dolphins had changed toward her in the past couple of months. But they couldn't know how important the Tadpoles were to her!

"Really, it wasn't like that at all, Mindy," she said miserably. She felt confused and somehow guilty. But working with the Tad-poles had been *right*, no matter what they said. Taking a deep breath, Megan managed to get her voice under control. "There weren't any special favors. Jeff told me that it would be OK if I worked with the Tadpoles on Wednesdays and Saturdays. . . ."

Her voice trailed off. There had been a lot

of practices scheduled for those days. And on Sundays, when the Tadpoles were running their afternoon races, she was helping them, not sailing with the Dolphins. Suddenly she could see why Louise and Mark and the others viewed Jeff's agreement as a special favor. Maybe if she and Jeff hadn't been dating, they would have felt differently about it. But maybe if she hadn't been his girlfriend, Jeff wouldn't have agreed to let her miss so much.

She stood still, trapped by her new knowledge. She had been right, but so had they. And Jeff had unexpectedly come to her rescue, trying to bring them all together again. Well, she owed it to him to help make the team one again. She swallowed hard. "Is there any way I can—can change the way Louise and the others feel about me?"

There was a long silence. "I don't know," Mindy said finally. "Jeff is pretty confident that everyone will begin to work together again. And as far as I'm concerned, that's the way it's going to be. But I think it's going to take some real effort on your part to prove that you're a dedicated member of the team."

Megan nodded with determination. Suddenly everything fell into place again. "You're right, Mindy. Jeff has gone out on a limb to help me. I'm going to make him glad he did."

The regatta committee met in the assembly hall. Megan had always liked the comfortable room. It had a low, beamed ceiling and a huge stone fireplace that bore the sooty stains from many winter-evening fires. Along one side of the room was a cedar-railed deck that faced a spectacular view of the lake, now almost lost in the warm June semidarkness. About twenty people were already gathered in friendly, noisy groups around the big worktable, which was scarred by many sail-mending and gear-repairing sessions.

Jeff was already there, deep in conversation with Gary at one side of the table. He moved over to make room for Megan. "Everything OK?" he asked her, grinning casually and reaching for her hand.

Megan felt her pulse flutter in her throat. Jeff had made sure that Louise and Mark stopped criticizing her. That proved how much he cared. "Everything's OK," she said softly, and Jeff let go of her hand and turned away.

Megan looked around the group. This was her first regatta committee meeting, and she wondered curiously who all the people were. Mr. Conrad waved from across the table. She knew and liked him. Carole had recruited him one afternoon to give a demonstration on water safety to the Tadpoles.

She saw Carole herself at the end of the table and smiled. Next to her was someone Megan didn't recognize, a dark-haired, tanned boy with sharply chiseled cheekbones and deep-set brown eyes. He was wearing, of all things, a dusty, sweat-stained black cowboy hat with a dirty, braided rawhide band. He wasn't exactly good-looking, but there was something interesting about him, and Megan found herself watching him. Perhaps it was his stillness, his quiet, watchful ease—nothing in the room seemed to escape his attention. For a moment he caught and held her glance and then slowly smiled. Surprised, Megan smiled back. Then the commodore stood up at the other end of the table, and everyone in the room stopped talking.

"Guess ya'll are wondering why I've called you here tonight," the commodore said in an exaggerated Texas drawl, and there was a ripple of laughter around the room. "As you know," he continued, "the Firecracker Regatta is the biggest event of the year for the

25

Cedar Lake Yacht Club, and it takes a heck of a lot of work from a heck of a lot of people to pull it off." Several people around the table, obviously experienced committee members, nodded to one another in agreement. "Some of us have been on the job for a couple of months already. It's time now to bring the rest of you folks up to date on our progress and get everybody on board for final assignments. Now, since we don't want to waste anybody's time, let's start off with a report from the committee on publicity. Pete, you out there somewhere?"

Mr. Conrad made the publicity report, and then there were reports from Mrs. Wilson, who was planning the barbecue that would take place on Saturday evening after the first day's races, from the people responsible for setting up the camping area, and from the standards committee, which would weigh the competing boats and measure their sails to be sure they met all the requirements. Finally, the commodore called on Jeff. "Where are we with the small-boat races?" he asked.

Jeff stood up. Megan always admired the comfortable, self-assured way he spoke in front of a group. He was never nervous or uncertain, the way she usually felt. "We'll be running a best-of-five series for Fireballs, Thistles, and Lasers," he reported. "We expect up to twenty boats in each of these classes, a total of about sixty."

"Made your work assignments yet?"

"Joe's handling race registration, and we've got four alternate race courses laid out. Everything's in pretty good shape, except that we're short on dock space again. We're not going to be able to handle a big turnout." He looked down the table and smiled confidently at Carole. "I thought maybe the Tadpoles could move over for a couple of days during the regatta and let us share their dock—or even let us use the whole thing. What do you say, Carole?" Megan looked up at Jeff in surprise. He hadn't told her about wanting to use the Tadpoles' dock.

But Carole was nodding as though the idea was a familiar one. "I don't think that will be a problem, especially if you need it for just a few days," she said thoughtfully. "But you'll have to work out the details with the new coach."

Megan's heart leaped to her throat, and she glanced at Carole swiftly, just in time to see her exchange a meaningful smile with the commodore. The boy next to Carole was leaning back in his chair, hands in his pockets, watching and listening attentively. He pushed a shock of dark, straight hair out of his eyes, and Megan noticed that his hands were thick and strong and calloused, probably from hours of work on boats. Maybe *he* was the new coach.

"Thanks for the report, Jeff," the commodore said. "OK, Dr. Daniels, let's hear from the course committee."

The rest of the evening went quickly as the other committees made their reports, but Megan didn't pay much attention. In spite of herself, she couldn't help wondering about the Tadpoles' new coach. *Oh well,* she thought, *I've already decided to devote the rest of the summer to the Dolphins, not the Tadpoles.*

After another ten minutes or so, the commodore distributed a handout. There was a general groan from the group around the table. "Don't panic, gang," the commodore said cheerfully. "This is just a checklist. Everybody work hard now, d'ya'll hear?"

"Look at that," Jeff muttered grumpily, pointing to the checklist. "Didn't I tell you? Dock clean-up duty. Campground patrol. More dirty work."

As everybody was leaving, the commodore called to Megan. "Would you mind staying for just a few minutes?" he asked. "I'd like to talk to you in my office."

"What's that about?" Jeff whispered.

Megan shook her head. "I don't know," she answered, but she had a dull, sinking feeling in the pit of her stomach. She could guess why the commodore wanted to see her. He was going to tell her about the Tadpoles' new coach. "I don't think this will take long," she said tensely. "Would you mind waiting?"

"No problem. But see if you can hurry it up. We want to stop at Maxwell's and get some ice cream. OK?" He touched her arm, and she looked up gratefully. Staring into his blue eyes, all thoughts of the Tadpoles melted away.

# Chapter Four

The commodore's desk was littered with papers and sailing charts, and a brass-plated antique compass kept a towering pile of papers from sliding onto the floor. Megan perched on the edge of a chair, and Carole sat on another. She smiled reassuringly at Megan as the commodore shuffled through the papers on his desk until he found what he wanted. In a minute he removed his glasses and polished them on the front of his shirt.

"Well, let's not waste any time," he began briskly in a businesslike voice. He put his glasses back on and peered over them at her. "The club has a proposition for you, Megan. I want to talk with you about a job."

"A job?"

"Yes. As you know, the only kids involved in the Tadpoles now are the children of club members. But sailing is a terrific sport for kids, and the club's board of directors would like to open it up to other children. That is, we'd like to develop a community sailing program for younger kids." He looked carefully at Megan, as if he were measuring her reaction.

"Now, we know that this won't be an easy program to manage," he went on, "and we suspect that it's going to be controversial. Some people think our junior sailing program ought to be limited to the children of yacht club members. But the board is determined to go on with this because they think there are so many benefits—for the club, as well as for the kids." He paused again. "Megan, we've decided you're the person we want. The board has authorized me to offer you the job of organizing the new program and coaching the Tadpoles."

Megan stared at him in amazement. "Me?" she cried, stunned. "You want *me* to coach the Tadpoles?" Suddenly she was incredibly happy.

"We couldn't find anybody better if we

interviewed a dozen people," Carole said, grinning broadly. "The kids really like you, and you'll be terrific at developing the new program. I hope you'll take the job."

"We can't think of anyone better qualified and more likely to be a success with the youngsters," the commodore said. "And you're very highly recommended by the best authority, the last coach." He paused, and there was a twinkle in his eye. "Oh, yes, I should tell you that the board has decided that the new coach should have a salary of three hundred dollars a month. Will you accept?"

Suddenly Megan remembered her earlier conversation with Mindy, and she felt as though she had been knocked down by an icy wave. If she took the coaching job, she might have to give up the Dolphins. But maybe she could convince Jeff that she could do both.

She took a deep breath. "I wish I could say yes this minute," she said raggedly, "but I have other obligations to consider. You see, there are the Dolphins—"

The commodore smiled understandingly. "Yes, I know how much your team depends on you. But don't you think that you and Jeff could work out some kind of compromise? I'm sure he'd understand."

He paused at the look on Megan's face and glanced quickly at Carole, who shook her head slightly. "Well, anyway, take a day or two to think about it. But do let me know in the next couple of days, OK?"

Megan nodded wordlessly, a hundred questions tumbling through her mind. But her lips felt numb, and she knew she would trip all over the words if she tried to say anything.

"And, Megan," Carole said softly, "let me know if I can help you think it through."

"Sure," Megan said. "And thanks again." It was all she could manage.

There was a long silence between Megan and Jeff during the drive to Maxwell's. In the backseat Gary and Mindy kept up a relaxed and lively conversation, but Jeff was busy concentrating on the sharp twists of the road in the heavy downpour that had begun just as they had left the clubhouse to dash to the car. Megan was glad to lose herself in the rainy darkness.

*I'll have to tell Jeff tonight,* she thought carefully, *and try to get him to understand that I can handle both. I know I can,* she told herself, chewing on her knuckle. But convincing Jeff wasn't going to be easy, and after what had happened that night, she certainly wasn't going to try it in front of Mindy and Gary.

She closed her eyes and wound her fingers together in her lap as she imagined Jeff's reaction. He would *have* to see how important this was to her. He'd definitely be upset for a little while, but then he'd understand.

"Hey, come on, Megan," Jeff said impatiently. Gary and Mindy were already out of the car and running across the parking lot toward Maxwell's, Cedar Springs' fantastic ice-cream parlor. But Megan was still sitting, looking out the window. "Would you rather sit out here in the dark by yourself, or are you going to come inside with the rest of us?" Jeff demanded.

Megan scrambled hastily out of the car. "Sorry," she mumbled apologetically as they jogged through the puddles. "Guess I wasn't paying attention."

"No lie," Jeff said dryly as they entered Maxwell's. "You and the commodore must really be cooking up something special. You

34

haven't said two words since you got in the car. What gives?"

"Oh, just some routine Tadpole stuff," Megan answered evasively. "Nothing important." She spotted Gary and Mindy settling into a booth in the far corner. "Come on, let's go."

As Jeff and Megan slid into the booth across from the other couple, Mindy looked at Megan inquisitively. "Well, aren't you going to tell us what the commodore wanted to talk to you about?"

"Oh, it wasn't anything important, just some stuff about the Tadpoles." Megan fumbled for something to add, wishing she could invent a believable reason for talking to the commodore. "He—he wanted to know about the dock."

"Oh, yeah?" Jeff raised his eyebrows and glanced pointedly at Gary. "Maybe we ought to hear about that. What did he want to know?"

Megan stammered. "He—he just asked about how crowded the Tadpole dock is and what kind of storage space is free. I—I guess he was asking because you raised the question tonight about the Dolphins needing dock space and—"

"You ready to order?" Pencil poised, the waitress stood over them, and Megan settled thankfully into her corner of the booth while they all ordered.

After the waitress left, Gary leaned across the table toward Jeff. "You know, Jeff, we've really got to do something about the dock space before the regatta. We just can't handle sixty boats off our dock."

Jeff waved his hand and smiled reassuringly. "Hey, no sweat. Why do you think I brought it up tonight? As soon as the new coach is on board, I'll make a deal to take over their dock for the regatta."

"Well, I don't know," Gary said doubtfully, glancing at Megan. "Doesn't look to me like the coach would see any advantage in moving the Tadpoles for those days. After all, the commodore assigned them to that dock to keep them out of the heavy traffic areas and so they'd have easy access to the lake." He leaned toward Megan. "What do you think the new coach is likely to do?"

Before she could answer, Jeff cut in confidently, "Megan's not involved with that bunch anymore. Just leave it to me. I've already got an idea that might sell them. And anyway, what's more important, the Tadpoles' playtime or running the regatta right? I'm willing to bet the commodore will see it my way even if the new coach doesn't agree. After all, it's a matter of priorities."

Feeling exhausted and a little sick, Megan leaned her head against the cool leather of the booth. She couldn't get Jeff's words out of her mind. "Megan's not involved with that bunch anymore" sounded over and over, like the lyrics from a stuck record. The two boys continued to talk excitedly about the upcoming regatta. They didn't even slow down when the waitress brought over their ice-cream sundaes.

"Hey, are you guys going to talk about sailing all night?" Mindy interrupted.

Gary pinched her arm affectionately. "Well, what do you propose? Shall we talk about waterskiing instead?"

"Very funny. Hey, did you notice that guy at the meeting tonight, the one sitting next to Carole?" She turned to Megan. "What did you think? Wasn't he cute?"

"I'm not sure I'd call him cute, exactly," Megan said slowly, thinking about the way he held himself, so confident, so self-assured. "But he was certainly different." For some reason, she didn't want to talk about him.

Jeff laughed sarcastically. " 'Different' is right." He cocked an imaginary cowboy hat over one eye and peered out under it with an exaggerated scowl. "Nobody, but nobody, wears a cowboy hat at the yacht club. If you're going to sail, you wear sailing clothes."

"But lots of guys wear cowboy hats all the time," Megan objected. "There's nothing strange about that." Now, why in the world was she defending someone she didn't even know?

"Not old beat-up hats stained with sweat and covered with dust," Jeff observed.

Megan suppressed a giggle, thinking about Jeff's snowy white cowboy hat with the shiny silver buckle and feather band, a far cry from the hat the dark-haired boy had worn.

"I'll tell you," Jeff continued, "that cowboy sure didn't look like much of a sailor. Wonder what he was doing at the meeting?"

"Maybe he's the new coach," Gary answered, stirring his sundae into a multiflavored puddle.

"Serve them right," Jeff said and grinned. "The little kids will do terrific with a cowboy for a skipper."

"He can skipper *my* boat any time he

wants," Mindy declared. She made a face at Gary and shoved a spoonful of hot fudge and whipped cream into her mouth.

"You mean I've been replaced by some mysterious drifter?" Gary demanded. "Mindy, honey, where's your loyalty?"

Laughing, Mindy pushed him playfully. Megan relaxed as the conversation flowed away from the Tadpoles onto the usual summertime topics. But she knew she was only postponing the talk with Jeff.

# Chapter Five

"Let's sit on the porch for a while," Megan suggested nervously as Jeff pulled the car up in front of her house after dropping Gary and Mindy off. The house was dark, and the porch light was on, so she knew that her mother wasn't home yet.

Jeff turned off the motor. "Yes, I think we need to talk."

Megan loved the old-fashioned wooden porch. The honeysuckle, growing along the side of the porch, blanketed the warm night with its heavy, sweet scent. The swing creaked familiarly when they sat down, and Megan tried to relax into its gentle sway. For a long time they sat silent, Jeff's arm along the back of the swing, the tips of his fingers lightly brushing her shoulder in a way that made her shiver. Finally, Megan broke the silence.

"Jeff, thanks for talking to Louise tonight."

Jeff half-turned toward her, dropping his hand. "I'm really concerned about the team, Megan." His voice was urgent. "We're just not working together the way we should be. I thought maybe it was because we were shorthanded—your being gone so much has really stretched us out—and I figured things would get better when you were back. But when Mark and Louise popped off tonight, I knew that if I didn't do something about it, we were just going to have more of the same old stuff. So I asked them to lay off."

"I know. Mindy told me. Thanks for—for defending me."

Jeff leaned forward and put his elbows on his knees, propping his chin in his hands. "Yeah, well, that's not quite the way it is. I'm responsible for the team's morale, and I can't let any of the members take advantage. I wasn't really defending you—it was the idea of everybody working together."

"Oh." Suddenly all the worries she'd had about Jeff and the Dolphins rushed back.

She felt as though something important had been taken away from her. "Well, thanks, anyway," she said lamely.

Jeff leaned back, his face withdrawn, distant. "You know, Megan, this—this cooperation thing goes both ways. I understand why some of the members of the team have been mad at you. They love to sail competitively. That's all they think about, all they talk about. And when they think you're not taking it seriously, they're bound to get mad."

Megan nodded. "I understand, but—"

Jeff interrupted her. "You're really important to the team, and we need you at every single practice. We just can't function without a full crew, especially with the regatta coming up."

"But don't you think—" Megan began, but Jeff kept on talking.

"It's especially unfair to Mindy. She's been counting on you for the Cedar Lake Cup this summer, and you've got to start practicing."

Megan took a deep breath. "There's something I have to tell you," she said almost in a whisper. She pulled her knees up to her chest and hugged her legs. She had to tell him now, before he said any more.

Jeff looked at her, his blue eyes narrowing intently. "What is it?"

She closed her eyes and said carefully, as though she were measuring every word, "The commodore offered me the job of coaching the Tadpoles." The thunder growled in the distance, and the rain suddenly poured down again.

"He wants you to do *what*?"

"The commodore and the board want to reorganize the Tadpoles and expand the program. And they want me to direct it."

"What's that supposed to mean, expand the program?"

"The board wants to get more kids involved in sailing, make the Tadpoles less exclusive. To do that, they want to turn it into a community sailing program with more kids and more activities. They've asked me to run it." She glanced at him silently, begging him to understand. "It's a chance for me to combine teaching and sailing, Jeff, and I really want to do it."

"But you can't!" Jeff stood up and looked down at her. His voice cut through the noise of the pounding rain. "The team is counting on you. *I'm* counting on you."

Megan looked over the rhododendrons

43

that lined the front of the porch, the lush green leaves shining in the dim light. "I know," she said quietly, putting her feet down on the floor. "And I don't want to let you *or* the team down."

"Well, isn't that reason enough for you to stay on with the Dolphins and let somebody else handle this—this community sailing program?" He sat down beside her and captured both of her hands in his, leaning so close that his breath brushed her cheek. "We've been—good friends, Megan," he whispered urgently. "More than good friends. Friends help each other out. And I need your help now. The Tadpoles can find another coach."

"But there's another way, Jeff. I can handle both the team *and* the Tadpoles if I plan it carefully."

Jeff shook his head firmly. "No way. Things have to go back to the way they were before you got involved in this other stuff. We had plenty of time for each other and the Dolphins then."

Megan looked down at their hands, his brown and strong ones holding hers with such authority. "I want to have time for you, Jeff," she whispered, trying to put into her voice all the love she felt for him. "But I need

44

to go on working with the kids. I can't tell you why I love it so much, but I do. Can't I practice with the team part of the time and race on weekends? I'm sure that one of the Tadpole parents could run the Sunday races."

Jeff dropped her hands and looked at her angrily. "You expect me to sell that idea to the team? I just told you that they resent all your missed practices."

"But don't you see—"

"It just won't work, Megan." He stood up abruptly, dropping her hands, and began to pace up and down. "They think I've been letting you miss some of the races just because we—we've been dating. So even if you *could* handle both jobs—which I doubt—the others wouldn't think it was fair. I've got to have a team where everybody trusts each other, where everybody works together."

Megan looked down at her hands. "Well, it looks like we're stuck." A flash of lightning lit up the porch with a harsh, blue and white glare, and the thunder nearly drowned out her words. "Either I give up this chance or I give up the team. Is that it?" She knew that there was one more choice to face, but she didn't want to be the one to say the words.

Jeff stopped and turned. "I guess that's

it," he said stonily. "But there's something else." Megan squared her shoulders and sat straighter. She knew what was coming. "If you decide that the coaching job is all that important, I don't think there's much left of our relationship."

Megan turned away. "I suppose I know how you feel," she whispered, her voice breaking. "But are you sure you understand how *I* feel?"

Jeff bent down and put his hand under her chin and tipped it up, looking deeply into her tear-filled eyes. "No, I guess I don't," he said. "For me, it'd be easy. I don't understand why you're even considering leaving the Dolphins—and splitting us up."

Megan fought back her tears, and after a minute she said, "You've given me a lot to think about." She stood up.

"I wish I could get inside your head and *make* you choose the right thing," Jeff said softly. "We need you, Megan. *I* need you."

He stepped toward her and put both his hands on her shoulders, kissing her quickly. Then he pulled her into his arms for a long, tender kiss that left her weak. He stepped back. "I'll bet that after you've sorted it all out, you'll decide that the team is more important—that *we're* more important—than this other thing. When you've decided that, let me know."

He turned quickly and walked out into the dark and the rain.

Megan was still sitting on the porch swing when her mother's car turned into the driveway. She decided to stay on the porch where it was dark so her mother wouldn't notice something was wrong and begin asking questions.

"Well, hello, dear." People often said that Megan and her mother looked alike, and Megan had to admit that there was a remarkable similarity in their gray eyes and upturned noses. They even had the same freckles; her mother thought that was cute. "What've you been up to tonight?"

"Not much," Megan answered, feeling trapped. There was also a startling similarity in the way they responded to problems, Megan thought, and her mother seemed to have an amazing ability to know when she was depressed or facing a big decision. "How did the catering go tonight?" she asked quickly before they could get on to the uncomfortable subject of *her* evening.

Mrs. Woods sighed, dropping onto the

swing next to Megan. "We had a big party, forty for cocktails and twenty for dinner. Things got kind of frantic about dessert time." She glanced at Megan. "We haven't had a chance to talk about your summer schedule. When can you start working for me?"

Megan couldn't help laughing. Of all things for her mother to ask that night! "My popularity these days is overwhelming," she said helplessly.

"Obviously that's supposed to mean something, but I'm afraid I'm not in on the joke. What's the secret?"

"It's kind of complicated."

"Since when has life been simple?" Mrs. Woods leaned back comfortably. "So what's up?"

Megan took a deep breath. "Well, the commodore has offered me the coach's job."

"Really? Oh, Megan, that's terrific! Isn't that exactly what you wanted?"

Megan nodded tiredly. "More, really. And the commodore even offered to pay me," she added, remembering how difficult it was for her mother's business right now. "It'd be good for my college fund. You could hire somebody else with the money you were going to pay me."

"Well, I knew you didn't want to come to work in the catering service, but I didn't know you'd go to *this* length to avoid it," her mother said, teasing. She gave her daughter an enthusiastic hug. "When do you start?"

Megan sighed and pulled away. "I wish it were that simple. Louise and Mark sounded off at me tonight about missing practice. And then Jeff made Louise apologize, but he wasn't really defending me. He couldn't—the team wouldn't—"

Her mother held up her hand. "Whoa. You've lost me somewhere. Try again, honey."

Megan took a deep breath and tried to control the despair she felt. "Jeff said I'd have to choose between sailing with the team and working with the Tadpoles. He said I couldn't do both."

"Well, that seems reasonable," Mrs. Woods said evenly. "I don't see how you could fit both those obligations into your schedule and still have time for the basics, like eating and sleeping." She watched Megan closely. "What else did he say?"

How did her mother always know the worst question to ask? "He said that if I decided to take the job we wouldn't—it would be the end. . . ."

The real meaning of Jeff's words suddenly crashed down on her. A chilly breeze had sprung up after the rain, and Megan shivered. "Mom, that means I won't be a part of the team anymore. And outside of that group, I don't have any friends! And even if Jeff and I have had a few problems lately, I still—love him." She'd never said those words out loud before, and somehow the sound of them made her realize how much she'd be losing. Suddenly the tears, hot and bitter, came rushing to her eyes. She buried her face in her mother's shoulder and sobbed. After a few minutes her crying subsided. She sniffled and took the tissue her mother offered her.

"Honey, this is a tough decision," Mrs. Woods said soothingly. She fished in her pocket for another tissue. "But maybe it's a good time in your life to be faced with it."

Megan glanced at her sharply. "I can't imagine that *any* time would be a good time."

"I just mean that since you've been a member of the team, you've really limited your circle of friends and your activities, too. The Dolphins seem awfully demanding to me, almost as if they don't trust one another to have any friendships outside their own tight little group." Mrs. Woods pushed the swing with her toe. "And they're a pretty exclusive group, too, with rather narrow interests—boats, sailing, swimming, parties. I haven't seen any of them holding down jobs or even doing volunteer work."

"But most of them don't *have* to work," Megan protested. "Their families are wealthy. They can afford to give them allowances and pay for college and buy boats. I'm not saying that's awfully important," she added hastily, thinking how hard her mother worked to keep things together for the two of them. "It's just the way it is."

"I know," her mother said, "that that's *exactly* the way it is. But devoting all your time to one group, especially one that's so narrow, is bound to make you narrow, too." She paused and then said quietly, "You know, one of the reasons for your father's and my divorce had to do with life-style, Megan. I just couldn't accept a life that was nothing but going to parties and spending money, and your dad and I couldn't agree on a different life-style that we could share. I had to go it alone—I had to be independent. For the first time in my life, I'm earning my own way." She sighed. "I don't think the divorce was the *only* way we might have worked things out, but as it turned out, both of us think it was the best way."

She turned to look at Megan closely. "It seems to me that you're being forced to make a decision, too, now that Jeff has posed your alternatives in such limited, either-or terms. Do you think his terms are fair?"

"Well, not exactly, but—"

"Would you have given Jeff an ultimatum like the one he gave you tonight?"

Megan thought for a moment. "No, I would have trusted him to work it out even if I had to defend his choice to the whole team. But on the other hand, the team is his whole life, and I can see why he feels the way he does. . . ." Her voice trailed off.

Mrs. Woods squeezed her hand sympathetically. "It's not too hard to choose between right and wrong. But it's awfully hard to choose between right and right. Sometimes it's just a matter of priorities." She stood up and held out both hands. "Now, how about some popcorn and cold cider?"

Megan stood up. She still wasn't ready to make a decision, but the problem seemed clearer now. "OK, as long as I make the popcorn. You look tired."

*Priorities.* Jeff had used that word, too. She sighed. The problem wasn't really with Jeff and the team because they already knew what their priorities were. The problem was with *her.* And now she had to decide on her priorities.

# Chapter Six

The storm had washed the sky clean, and the late morning sun was bright and warm as Megan drove toward the lake. She was on her way to see the commodore to tell him she was taking the job. Like a magic potion, the popcorn and cider had put her to sleep the night before, and when she'd woken up, she knew what to do.

Although her decision was made, she felt like crying when she thought of losing Jeff. Now, driving down the narrow lane that led through the fragrant cedar trees to the lake, Megan tried to put Jeff and the Dolphins out of her mind. Working with the Tadpoles, organizing the new sailing program, planning new events for a larger and more diverse group of kids—these were all exciting, and she couldn't help but look forward to her new responsibilities.

The commodore was posting notices on the outdoor bulletin board when Megan drove up, and as they walked into the clubhouse together, she told him she was accepting the job of coach for the Tadpoles.

"I'm glad you've decided to help us with the program, Megan," he said warmly. "We need you and your ideas. And the kids will be very pleased." And then, almost as an after-thought, he added, "Did you and Jeff settle on an arrangement with the Dolphins?"

Megan hesitated and then spoke as brightly as she could. "We don't think we can work it out, so Jeff will be looking for somebody to take my place. I'm sure he'd appreciate it if you'd pass the word around."

There was a silence, and then the commodore said slowly, "I'm sorry you couldn't make it work. But I'm glad you've agreed to manage the Tadpole program." Megan was glad, too, except when she thought about Jeff. "I'd like to hear your ideas about the things that have to be done before we start recruiting," the commodore said. "But it's such a beautiful morning, let's have a cup of coffee on the deck instead of shutting ourselves into the office."

From the deck that ran along the side of the assembly hall, the lake looked still and calm. "It's beautiful," Megan agreed, "but there's not much wind. I'm glad the kids aren't here today. We'd have to spend our time paddling."

For the next half hour, they talked about ideas for the expanded program. The commodore suggested eventually doubling the current size of the group. They discussed new activities, ways to interest children in the community, recruiting strategies, equipment needs. The more they talked, the more excited Megan became. She could see that the success of the new program was going to depend largely on her creativity and resourcefulness. But at the same time, she could see that if the program was going to be accepted, other people would have to get involved in the project.

"We need to set up an advisory board," she said thoughtfully. "Maybe some parents should belong to it. So could the directors of other community programs like the YMCA.

And of course, we need some people from the club."

"Hey, that's a good idea," the commodore said enthusiastically. "The more people who become a part of it, the more people will support the idea. I think Pete Conrad would like to help out. And the advisory board could help you locate some of the equipment you'll need. Now, what about the dinghies? What's your situation there?"

Sipping her coffee, Megan considered. "We've got about a dozen usable dinghies stacked against the dock, and there are a couple that need work behind the repair shed. We also need more storage space."

The commodore looked thoughtful. "And what about the dock space? Seems to me you'll be a little crowded with another dozen kids out there."

Megan laughed shortly, thinking about Jeff's plan to take over the Tadpoles' dock. "Yes, we'll have to think about some alternatives. One thing is sure; if we're going to add a dozen kids, we can't afford to share any of our space with the Dolphins."

The commodore glanced at her sharply and was about to say something, but he was interrupted by a shrill whistle from below.

Megan leaned over the railing. Standing on the terrace, squinting up at them, was the boy she had seen at the meeting the night before.

"Hey, Commodore, I'm ready to drive into town for the supplies to repair the winch," he called. "Do you need anything?" His voice was deep and strong, with a slow Texas drawl.

"Come on up before you go, Ben. There's someone here I want you to meet."

His name was Ben Holliday, Megan learned when the commodore introduced them, and he'd been hired to help the grounds crew maintain the club grounds and buildings. During the week he lived alone in the little house trailer behind the boat repair shed, and in the fall he would be a freshman at the state university.

"Working here gives me a cheap place to live while I'm going to school," he said to Megan when the commodore finished introducing them. He grinned and Megan noticed how bright his teeth were in contrast to his tanned face. "And besides, I really like working with my hands. By now, I'm pretty good at it."

The commodore laughed and slapped Ben's shoulder. "That's the understatement of the year. In the few days he's been here, he's repaired plumbing, patched a roof, and now he says he can fix the winch problem that's baffled every expert for the last three months. We think he's a real winner."

"Pleased to meet you, Ben." Megan smiled.

"Ben, Megan is the new director of our Tadpole program. Until now, the program has involved sailing lessons and races for kids from the club. But the board has decided to expand it and make it a little less exclusive. Megan has agreed to recruit another dozen kids and develop some new activities. You'd be the perfect person to help her plan and build some new wooden lockers and maybe an extension on the boat rack. And would you check the repair shed? There are also a couple of dinghies there that we ought to put back in service."

"Sounds good," Ben said, nodding. "If you've got time, we can take a look at the dock this morning so I can order the supplies."

"Why don't you two do that right now?" the commodore suggested. "Megan, if you'll make a list of the new activities you've got in mind, I'll be glad to go over them with you in a day or two."

Megan smiled gratefully. "That would be a big help. I'm glad that you're giving me all this responsibility, but it scares me a little to think about developing a whole new program by myself. I'll feel a lot more comfortable if you'll look over my ideas."

"Glad to," the commodore agreed. "Now, let's get to work."

As she and Ben walked toward the dock, Megan glanced sideways at Ben. A wide leather belt heavy with carpenter's tools was slung low around his slim hips, his worn khaki shirt was open at the throat, and the sleeves were rolled to the elbows showing his brown arms. He wasn't much taller than she was, but his shoulders looked broad and muscular under his shirt. His jeans were tucked into the dusty tops of stained and battered cowboy boots, and his cowboy hat was pushed to the back of his head. Megan thought of Jeff's cutting remark and of Jeff's own flower-print cowboy shirt and spotless silver-buckled cowboy hat.

"How do you like living here all by yourself?" she asked curiously. "Doesn't it ever get lonely?" The minute the question was out of her mouth she wished it back again. It sounded so personal. But Ben didn't seem to notice.

"Not really." He glanced back at her as he

led the way down the stairs. "I've got Dog for company and Truck for getting away. Most weekends I go home to help Mom at the ranch." He pointed down. "Watch out. Step's loose."

"Who's Dog?" Megan asked.

Ben gave a loud whistle, and a small brown dog dashed out of the bushes along the shore and stopped short, head tipped curiously.

"That's Dog," Ben explained cheerfully. "Mostly mutt, but a good watchdog and great company. Truck is parked around back. She's mostly mutt, too, but cheap and reliable and easy to fix. But what about you? You must be one of those boat-people if you're going to run the Tadpole program."

Megan nodded. "I've been helping Carole with the program for the last couple of months. But I've been sailing for most of my life. What kind of boat do you sail?" *Probably one named* Boat, she thought, smiling to herself.

Ben laughed, a deep, unself-conscious laugh that seemed to match his rich Texas drawl. "Me? Heck, I don't sail. I'm just a ranch hand and a carpenter. The only kind of boats I know anything about are the kind you go fishing in." They had reached the dock, and

Ben looked around. "Now, suppose you show me what we need to do here."

They spent the next half hour discussing different places to build new lockers, storage sheds, and boat racks. Ben seemed to understand exactly what Megan wanted and made several suggestions for better ways to use the space.

"If you're going to put another dozen kids into this area, you're going to need more room," he said thoughtfully. He paced off the length of the dock. "You've only got thirty feet here. That means you can't tie up more than eight or nine boats at a time without a lot of confusion and bumping. Right?"

"I thought you said you've never been around sailboats," Megan said in surprise.

"You don't have to be an expert sailor to be able to figure out how much space you need to rig a boat," Ben answered, and Megan felt her face flushing.

"Yes, when we get more than eight boats lined up here, the kids start falling all over themselves. That's dangerous."

"Well, then, we'll need to come up with an answer if you're going to expand the program. But that can wait for a day or two. For now, let's get that shed put up and your lockers built." He glanced curiously at her. "Ever handle a hammer?"

Megan lifted her chin. "Of course," she said with more confidence than she felt. "I built a shelf in my bedroom last summer."

He grinned, and a dimple showed at the corner of his mouth. The grin warmed his eyes and made him look very young. "I hope you got it up straight. In a lot of ways, a shelf is harder to handle than a shed. A shed has four walls to hold it up. A shelf's only got one."

Megan laughed. "It isn't exactly level," she admitted, "but at least nothing falls off it."

"Good. Then I'll fix you up with some tools, and you can lend a hand on this project." He stopped to calculate, his dark eyes narrowing with concentration. "Let's see, I figure we can get started tomorrow or the next day. How does that sound?"

"Great," Megan said happily. "Just let me know when you're ready."

"Sure will," Ben said and grinned. Then he sauntered up the stairs toward the clubhouse, Dog trotting along behind him. Megan followed him with her eyes until he was out of sight.

\*     \*     \*

As much as Megan missed Jeff, she didn't have much time to think about him during the next few days. She was too busy preparing activities and thinking up ideas for the commodore, as well as fulfilling the usual responsibilities for the Tadpole program.

On Wednesday she met the kids at the dock and made them sit around her while she perched on one of the dinghies. "OK, gang, quiet down," she said sternly, frowning at Tod, the self-appointed leader, who seemed to be trying to tie Suzie's wrists with a length of rope. Obediently Tod dropped the rope and sat down cross-legged; the others followed his example. "I've got an announcement to make," she said, watching their faces carefully, "about the new coach."

Pam, who was sitting next to her twin sister Sam, held up her hand. "Do we get to vote?" she asked anxiously. A wave of laughter swept the group, but several still looked worried.

"Nope, no voting," Megan answered firmly. "I hope you're all going to be happy to hear that the commodore asked me to take over the Tadpole program."

At that the kids let out a shout of delight that echoed across the cove. "Really truly?"

Sam exclaimed, jumping up to give Megan a damp hug. "You're the one we wanted to vote for!"

"Really truly?" Megan echoed happily. She hugged Sam back. "I'm glad you're glad because I am, too. Now, I've got some other news," she said, and she told them about the commodore's plan to expand the sailing program. "In the new program a lot more kids will be able to learn to sail, and you'll make some new friends," she concluded. "I know that it will change what you're used to, but I hope that you'll help us make it a good change. It won't happen all at once. We're going to bring the new kids in a few at a time. With your help everything will go just fine."

After ten minutes of questions and answers, the kids seemed pleased with the idea that their program was going to include some new people. A few even asked whether they could help with the new sailors.

"Of course," Megan answered enthusiastically. "We can develop a buddy system in which each of you old sailors can show one of the new ones the ropes. Anybody have any other good ideas?" There was more excited discussion about how to bring new members into the group, and then Megan interrupted. "We've got lots of time to work on the new program, gang. Now, we need to get sailing. Everybody ready?"

Megan had announced capsize drills, so everybody had worn swimsuits. After a long, hard drill, she was pleased with their progress, and at five-thirty, wet but happy, she blew her whistle.

"OK, kids," she called out. "Everybody in."

The sails had to be spread out to dry in the warm, late-afternoon sun, and a couple of boats had to have minor repairs, so it was late by the time Megan was ready to leave. She was sitting quietly on the dock, watching the water turn golden in the sunset, when she saw that the Dolphins had hoisted their sails and were going out for a late-evening practice—or perhaps for a nighttime picnic at Surprise Island. Each boat had both a skipper and a crew member, so she knew with a sinking heart that she'd already been replaced. It probably shouldn't have upset her. But she couldn't help feeling regret as she watched them sail while she was left alone on shore. After all, she still cared for Jeff, and the Dolphins were still her only friends, or used to be.

For a moment she wasn't sure what to do. They were going to sail close to the dock. Should she hurry up the stairs in order to be gone by the time they drew near? She glanced toward the first boat tacking toward her. Jeff was at the helm, and Mindy was crewing for him, both laughing happily as they tacked in her direction. It was too late to leave. They would think she was running away.

She bent over and pretended to be busy with something in the sail locker, looking up just as Jeff's Fireball skimmed past. "Hi," she called, waving casually. But neither Jeff nor Mindy looked in her direction, and the rest of the team, following Jeff's lead, chattered noisily as they sailed past. Nobody waved.

When they'd gone, Megan sat down and stared across the lake. Jeff's boat, its sail a bright triangle against the dusky sky, tacked twice, still leading the rest of the fleet, and headed toward Surprise Island. So they weren't going out for a practice race that night. Instead, they'd build a big fire on the beach, cook hot dogs, roast marshmallows, and listen to music.

*Jeff and Mindy,* Megan thought dully. *They couldn't wait to pair up, could they?* And as she drove home that evening, Megan felt uncertain about herself. Being one of the Dolphins had made her feel special; now she was just ordinary Megan Woods again. Giving up her place on the team, losing Jeff—it was almost like losing her identity. She wondered if she'd made the right choice.

# Chapter Seven

For the next week Megan put all her energy into the Tadpoles. It was exciting and fun, and she felt a real sense of accomplishment as she watched the program take shape. Besides, it kept her mind off the Dolphins— and Jeff and Mindy. She told herself not to let it get to her. *At least,* she thought, remembering the way everybody had sailed past the dock without even a wave, *don't let them see how much it hurts.* But the hurt deepened every time she saw the Dolphins working on their boats or glimpsed Jeff and Mindy sailing together. But she spent so much time at the yacht club, there was no way to avoid it.

The work with the Tadpoles was even

more challenging than she had expected. Megan had placed an ad in the *Cedar Springs Herald* inviting applications for three new places in the Tadpole program. There were twice as many applications as she expected, and the three places were filled immediately by children whose parents could never have afforded club memberships. One of the new kids was an excellent swimmer and a good athlete and took to sailing immediately. But the other two were going to need a lot of attention, and after careful thought, Megan decided to assign Pam and Sam as their buddies. She was delighted at the confident way the twins took charge.

But there was more to do than work with new members of the program. Megan met with the commodore in his office two weeks after their first meeting and explained the details of the junior sailing demonstration she wanted to show at the regatta. The kids would perform various sailing moves that would show off what they'd learned. They also discussed Megan's sailing program. She'd decided to base it on a series of progressively harder lessons, each one introducing a new concept in sailing. The lessons, which would cover a three-week period, would also leave plenty of time for the kids to learn water safety, grasp the basics of sailing equipment and rigging, and gain a basic understanding of weather and wind conditions.

"Who do you think I could get to help me out in the specific areas?" she asked the commodore.

"Doc Daniels would be happy to work out some presentations on weather and wind. Pete Conrad has already volunteered on water safety, and Jeff would probably be willing to do a couple of sessions on sailing equipment."

Megan shook her head. "I'd rather find somebody else to handle the equipment demonstrations," she said, not looking up.

"Still haven't settled your differences?" the commodore asked gently.

"No. And it doesn't look like we're going to. They've already found somebody to take my place." At the commodore's quizzical look she added carelessly, "Oh, I'm not upset or anything. I know it was just a matter of priorities. Jeff needs to keep the team working together and winning."

"I see," the commodore said steadily. "Well, it looks as though you have more than enough to keep you busy, anyway, especially with the demonstration coming up. And how are you and Ben getting along with the repair work?"

"That's going just fine," Megan said, smiling for the first time during the conversation. "In fact, I've got to meet him on the dock right now. We're just finishing the new storage shed he designed." Megan reached for her gear bag. "So, thanks for talking to me about my ideas."

"My pleasure, Megan. The program looks like it's going to be excellent," the commodore answered.

Megan smiled happily to herself as she headed for the dock. The commodore had approved all her plans. And she had a morning of work with Ben to look forward to.

Much to her surprise, Megan had discovered that helping Ben with the repair and building projects was even more fun than working with the Tadpoles. The two of them met about nine in the morning and worked until two, with a break for sandwiches, which Megan brought from home.

Megan was really enjoying the hours she spent with Ben learning new skills. Ben was an incredibly patient teacher, and although he sometimes made her repeat something twice or three times until she got it right, he always made her feel that her efforts were worthwhile and that he really needed her help.

"Hey, Ben," Megan called from the top of the stairs overlooking the dock, "sorry I'm a little late. I was talking to the commodore." She jogged down the steps.

"So, what happened?" Ben asked, pushing his cowboy hat back on his head. "Did he like your ideas?"

"Sure did. Oh, Ben, I'm so excited."

"I knew you'd do a great job," he replied with a smile.

"You and me together. I'd never be able to handle a bigger program without all the new storage space you've built."

"We've built." Ben corrected her. "You and me together."

Megan smiled. "OK, we've built." Then she looked serious.

"Are you going to study engineering when you go to college next year?" she asked.

Ben laughed. "You mean you think I ought to be an engineer just because I like to build things? No, I'm more interested in teaching." He paused for a moment to think, then added, "I'd like to teach in a junior high, probably carpentry and woodwork. When kids make things with their hands, it helps them feel better about themselves. I know *I* do." He turned to her, shading his dark eyes with his hand, smiling the familiar lopsided smile she had grown to like. "Isn't that why you're teaching these kids to sail?"

Megan was quiet for a moment. "I hadn't thought about it that way," she said, "but I guess you're right. What I like best about working with the kids is seeing how they change, even in a short time. They love to learn, and when they can show off what they know, they're really proud of themselves."

"There you go," Ben said, grinning. "You're a good teacher, Megan. You help kids learn without calling attention to what they don't know."

Megan blushed happily. "Speaking of teaching," she said quickly, "I wonder if you'd like a sailing lesson. You said you'd never been out in a sailboat, and since you think I'm a good teacher, maybe you'd be willing to trust yourself to me for a couple of hours."

"You're on." He looked down at his feet. "But I'll bet you won't let me wear my boots on the boat."

"No way." Megan laughed. "Shorts and sneakers. No boots, no cowboy hat."

"No cowboy hat?" Ben laughed. "Why,

that's like giving Dog away or trading Truck for a newer model! Do you expect me to abandon all my old friends just because you've got this narrow-minded notion about the right thing to wear sailing?" Still laughing, he ducked when Megan reached out and tried to grab his hat.

But the next day, to her surprise, Ben showed up at the dock in a pair of ragged cut-offs and sneakers—and without his cowboy hat. "Gosh," she said teasingly, "you look just like a regular person."

"Cut the cracks, teacher, and let's get going," he said firmly. "It's schooltime."

It was a beautiful day, clear and cloudless, with a stiff breeze that filled the sails and heeled the little boat over sharply. "You have to sit up here on the windward side and lean out," Megan explained. "Our weight counterbalances the force of the wind against the sail and keeps the boat at just the right angle. It's called hiking."

To demonstrate, she hooked her toes under the straps in the bottom of the boat and leaned back flat so the boat stood straighter. Quickly Ben did the same, and with his weight as a balance, Megan could sit up a little and adjust the sails and the tiller. The dinghy wasn't as fast as Jeff's Fireball, but it was a good little boat, and they sailed quickly across the lake.

"Now, we're going to try a tack," Megan said. "That means we catch the wind in the other side of the sail. When I say 'Ready about,' you uncleat this line. It controls the sail at the front of the boat. Then the boom will swing around as the nose of the boat turns across the wind. You'll have to duck. Then cleat the jib sheet so it stays steady on the other side of the boat and hike out."

Ben picked up the end of the line. "You call this a sheet?" he asked curiously.

Megan grinned. "I'll bet that's the most confusing term in sailing. Everybody thinks a *sail* ought to be called a sheet because it looks like a bed sheet. But the sheet is the line you have in your hand, and it's attached to the sail. Got it?"

"Got it," Ben responded. And with a "Ready about," Megan pushed the helm down sharply, and the boat swung onto the new tack.

"Great!" she said enthusiastically when Ben had pulled in the sail tightly and cleated the line and they were headed back across the lake. "Now, take the tiller and try it for yourself."

Ben took Megan's place as she moved forward to hike out. It was blowing harder now, and whitecaps were beginning to break across the tops of the waves. "Those white-caps mean that the wind is blowing about eighteen knots," she said. "Now we're *really* going to move fast."

Megan had expected Ben to be a little uneasy, especially when the wind started to blow harder, but he seemed to have an in-stinctive feel for the boat. Every few minutes Megan showed him a different sail set, and by the time they'd tacked upwind a dozen times, she was sure he could handle the boat all by himself.

"All you need is practice," she told him happily. "You're a natural. You've got a feel for it that very few people have even after they've sailed a lot."

"Too bad I won't have more time for sailing," Ben answered. "Next week I've got to help renovate the boat repair area and build a new hoist."

"But what about weekends?" Megan de-manded. "You don't work all day Saturday and Sunday, do you?"

Ben grinned at her. "Yep. But not here. At the ranch. I've got a couple of special projects I'll show you sometime. Still, if you'll come out with me, I'll try to fit in an hour or so of sailing a week."

"But you're such a good sailor. You really ought to spend more time with it!" Megan exclaimed impatiently. "You could be winning races with just a couple of weeks hard practice! You could be even better than Jeff!"

Ben patted her arm and smiled crookedly. "Thanks, teacher, but I'm not interested in competing with Jeff—on the race course or anywhere else. There are too many other things to do in this world." He threw her a look she couldn't read. "Ever been to a rodeo?"

"A rodeo?" Megan asked in surprise. What an unexpected change of subject! "No, I haven't. But," she added quickly, "it might be interesting." She wasn't sure that it *would* be interesting, actually, but she didn't want to offend Ben by saying so.

"OK, I'll trade you one rodeo for one sailing lesson," he said promptly. Just then the wind shifted, and they both had their hands full for the next twenty minutes.

Ben didn't say any more about the rodeo as they docked the boat and put the sails away. He just thanked Megan for the afternoon and went off to run some errands. But Megan couldn't put his puzzling comment out of her mind. What in the world had he meant when he said he didn't want to compete with Jeff?

# Chapter Eight

Megan was so busy that she didn't have much time to dwell on the hurt she felt whenever she saw Jeff and Mindy together or when one of the Dolphins snubbed her. The sharp, painful unhappiness was fading into a dull, distant ache. In fact, she was beginning to feel comfortable with herself for the first time in ages.

But a day or two after Ben's sailing lesson, everything flip-flopped, and Megan wasn't sure what to think. She'd just finished a lesson on boat rigging with the Tadpoles, a difficult topic. They all wanted to sail boats, not talk about them. After the kids had left and she was stowing the gear, she heard a familiar whistle. She looked up in surprise. It was Jeff, leaning nonchalantly against the shed she and Ben had built, looking more handsome and more sure of himself than ever.

"Hello, Megan," he said gravely. "It's good to see you."

Her heart thumping, Megan turned away and continued coiling the lines, trying to concentrate on what her hands were doing. "I thought today was your regular sailing practice," she said briefly.

"We had a work session on the regatta instead. Everybody's getting ready for the big day. Are the Tadpoles doing anything special?"

"We're planning a sailing demonstration here in the cove during the afternoon while the races are going on." She knew her voice didn't sound very friendly, but how else could she answer?

Jeff came closer and sat down on the hull of an overturned boat, watching her while she worked. After a long silence he caught her glance and held it, his blue eyes soft. "I've missed you, Megan."

Megan felt shocked. "But I see you and Mindy sailing together every day," she said slowly. "I thought—"

"Well, don't." Jeff's voice went hard. "We're

just trying out different combinations of skippers and crew members, to see if we can do any better." He picked up a length of line and began to tie a monkey's fist knot at one end of it. Suddenly he dropped the line. "Would you go to a movie with me tonight?" he asked suddenly.

"To-tonight?" Megan stammered. She took a deep breath, trying to match Jeff's matter-of-fact tone of voice. "Yes, I'd like to," she said quietly. But inside her heart was rejoicing in this sudden turnaround. *He still cares about me!* she cried to herself. *How could I have been so wrong?* She was happier than she'd ever been in her life. Surprisingly, Ben flashed into her mind. But she pushed his image away. *Tonight is going to be special,* she told herself.

Megan wore her new pink-striped blouse and the pair of designer jeans she'd bought with her first paycheck. Jeff took her to a movie in Lake Hills, and afterward they stopped at Maxwell's. They sat at a table in the back corner, and although a couple of members of the team came in and waved, no one came over. Megan relaxed, glad for the chance to be close to Jeff again, feeling warm waves of contentment wash over her.

Jeff smiled and reached for her hand. "Happy?" he asked.

"Yes," Megan answered simply. There weren't words to describe how happy she felt. "You?"

"Sure thing," he said casually, squeezing her hand briefly. He dropped it quickly, and Megan felt vaguely disappointed, as though there ought to be more.

*But this is still so new,* she thought. *We both need time to get used to each other again.* She considered telling Jeff about some of the Tadpoles' new activities, but things were going so smoothly she hated to mention anything that might upset the easy closeness of the evening. So they ate their ice cream in comfortable silence. Megan was so delighted to be with Jeff again that she didn't even ask herself—or him—why he had changed his mind so suddenly.

After Maxwell's Jeff drove Megan back to her house. "Want to sit on the porch for a little while?" she asked. "Mom made some lemonade."

"Great," Jeff said enthusiastically. "Your mom's lemonade is the best."

Megan brought out two tall, icy glasses of lemonade, and they sat together on the porch swing, chatting about the summer's activities. Jeff seemed to be going out of his way to fill her in on the details of the team's plans for the regatta, and she felt complimented that he wanted her to know what was going on. She leaned back dreamily and listened to the sound of his voice, hardly even paying attention to his words.

"And so we've got an even bigger list of entrants than we thought," he was saying, "almost seventy-five boats, fifteen more than we planned for."

"I guess Joe's publicity plan was almost *too* successful, from that point of view," she said, sipping her lemonade.

Jeff sat back and crossed his arms across his chest. "Yeah, I guess so," he said glumly. "We've been trying to decide what to do about the dock situation, and there doesn't seem to be a good answer." Turning toward her, he put his arm across the back of the porch swing. He let it slip around her shoulder, and she could feel his warmth through her thin blouse. "Megan, we've been talking again about using the Tadpoles' dock." He hesitated, then blurted out, "Do you think we could make a deal?"

"A deal?" Megan's heart turned over.

"What we'd like to do is use your dock." Quickly, at the look on Megan's face, he raised his hand. "Just for the regatta, I mean. We've *got* to have extra space, and your dock is bigger than ours, and it's in a much better position. I thought we could—"

Megan didn't let him finish. She stood up, eyes flashing angrily. "You mean you thought you could manipulate me into agreeing to a—a *deal* by telling me how much you missed me, taking me to a movie, and buying me ice cream. And all you wanted was to take over my dock." Furiously, she fought down a sob. "Did you really think I'd be dumb enough to fall for your horrible little trick?"

"It wasn't a trick," Jeff protested hotly. "I did want to see you again. I *have* missed you. We were so—good together, and I still want us to go back to the way we were before you started this other thing. But if we can't do that, at least maybe we can be partners. The Dolphins *need* that space, Megan. You said a month ago you wanted to help by being a member of the team. Well, that hasn't worked out. But you can make an even more important contribution by—"

"By letting you take over our dock. Is that it? Well, Jeff Freeman, if that's your idea of how to make a contribution, you can just find somebody else to be your—your *partner*." And with that Megan turned and fled into the house so that Jeff couldn't see the tears flowing down her cheeks.

Even hours later Megan could still taste the angry tears. How could Jeff have done such a thing? How could he have let her think, for that brief, marvelous time, that they could get together again? When she thought about it, she became angry all over again. But there was nothing to do except go on. *At least,* she told herself gratefully, *I have the Tadpoles to keep me busy. Even if I don't have any friends, I have more than enough work to do.*

And there *was* a lot of work. She and Ben had finished repairing the dock, but, at Ben's suggestion, they decided to add a bench along one side of the dock with storage underneath for the kids' life jackets. So the two of them, with the help of three older Tadpoles, spent several extra days sawing and hammering and painting.

The day they finished, the commodore came down to the dock for a look. "Fantastic, Megan," he said approvingly. "You've done a first-rate job on the renovations."

"Thanks," she answered shyly, "but most of the credit belongs to Ben. He designed the whole thing."

"He's certainly a talented young man. I'll be sure to thank him when I see him. By the way, how's the program coming along?"

Megan smiled proudly. "Just fine. I have six new Tadpoles signed on for the second series of lessons. Since my first class will graduate at the regatta, I'd like to give them certificates when we hand out the trophies for the races. Is that OK?" The commodore nodded, and Megan went on, "Then I'll start recruiting for the third session. A couple of the club members have volunteered to give some new demonstrations."

"I'm glad that you're involving other club members, Megan. You know, I told you in the beginning that there was opposition to the idea of opening up the Tadpoles to nonmember children. And your efforts to include people have really paid off. We haven't heard any of the negative comments about the program that we expected—thanks to you."

Megan blushed with pleasure. "I'm glad things are working out."

"There's one more thing I want you to think about," the commodore said sternly.

"What's that?"

"Now that the Tadpoles are developing so well, we need to talk about ways to use the Dolphins to help with the program. If they would give you a hand a couple of times a week, you could offer more personalized attention and many more activities."

A deep, hot resentment rose to Megan's throat. "I—I don't think that would work," she said, turning away. "The Dolphins are pretty busy with their racing."

"I know," the commodore said. "But that's just the point. The team has limited itself to competitive sailing—they should be doing more. You could help them change that."

Megan shook her head stubbornly. "What they do is their business."

The commodore looked at her intently. "I understand that you want the Tadpoles all to yourself, Megan," he said carefully. "In a way, you should, since you've done so much to build up the new program. But you can let the Dolphins give you a hand without losing control. You don't need to be jealous of their help."

Megan turned blankly to him. What in the world was he talking about? "Jealous?" she said incredulously. "You think I want to keep the Tadpoles separate because I'm *jealous*?"

The commodore smiled gently. "Well, let's just say that you don't seem very willing to share the program with Jeff or any of the Dolphins." He patted her shoulder. "Anyway, it's something for you to think about. I'm not asking you to commit yourself to it right away."

"Yes, sir," she answered flatly. But inside, Megan burned with anger. *I'll never commit the Tadpoles to that kind of arrangement,* she thought. *Never.*

# Chapter Nine

Ben seemed to realize that Megan was un-
happy, and he went out of his way to cheer
her up. He stopped at the dock nearly every
day to show the kids how to make simple
repairs to the boats. Early one evening, just
as Megan was finished cleaning up the gear,
he came down the stairs to the dock. His
black hair was carefully combed, and he was
wearing a white shirt, open at the neck. His
jeans were clean and neat, his boots were
shined, and even his old black cowboy hat
looked spruced up.

"Ready?" he asked Megan.

"Ready for what?" She leaned over and
gave one of the boats a last swipe with her
sponge.

"Rodeo time," Ben said and smiled. "Remember our deal? One rodeo for one sailing lesson."

"Tonight?" she gasped. "But—but—I have to call Mom."

"OK, but I know she'll approve," he said firmly, reaching for her hand. "Good clean Texas fun. You'll love it."

The rodeo was held at the fairgrounds in a huge barnlike arena with rows of wooden bleachers around three sides. The center was enclosed with high metal fences, and the entire floor was covered with nearly a foot of soft dirt. High against the wall at one end was the announcer's stand draped in red, white, and blue bunting. Beneath it was a confusion of what looked like crazily zigzagging fenced paths.

"Those are the livestock chutes," Ben said after they had settled in the bleachers with enough hot dogs and popcorn for the whole night. "The animal is held tightly by the chute so it can't move around. Then the cowboy drops down onto its back, and the handlers open the gate. We're just in time for the bucking bronco event, and that looks like Pete

Miller. He's a terrific rider. Now watch what happens when he drops onto Old Thunder."

Megan watched, fascinated, as the gate to chute number four was pulled open and a sorrel horse exploded into the arena. A cowboy was gripping its back with his legs, spurred heels lifted against the horse's muscular shoulders, one arm flung high for balance. Stiff-legged, the horse bucked furiously, hind legs kicking high. Little puffs of dirt spurted up under its pounding hooves.

"Wow," Ben said admiringly, "that's some ride Pete's getting!"

In less than ten seconds it was all over. The pickup rider, a man in jeans and a blue satin shirt, rode alongside the bucking horse. Pete Miller swung easily onto the pickup horse, and another rider corralled the free bronc and herded it easily back through the gate.

"You've seen a real champ," Ben said. "The rider's got to stay on the horse for eight seconds, and he can use only one hand. If he touches the horse with his free hand, he's out."

"How do you know who wins?" Megan asked curiously.

"Well, it's a partnership between the rider and the horse," Ben said, laughing. "You hope you get a tough horse because a more difficult horse gets higher points. And you're scored on your ability to time your spurring action with the bucking pattern of the horse."

Megan shook her head. "It looks hard," she said.

"Right. Most people think that bull riding is more dangerous than bronc riding, but it's not true. Bailing off one of these fellas is an experience you won't forget. That dirt may look soft, but it sure isn't."

Although the riding events were the most exciting, there was much more to watch, Megan discovered. There was the rodeo clown. Wearing a colorful cape and a big sombrero, he danced out in front of the angry bulls. "Jake may look like a clown," Ben commented, "but he's got the serious job of distracting the bull from a thrown rider. He's an expert animal handler, and he's got a lot of guts."

"How do you know so much about the rodeo?" Megan asked. "You even know a lot of the performers."

Ben smiled and handed her another hot dog. "I rodeoed last summer," he answered, "and every now and then I get the urge again. My little brother Bill is entering the calf roping at the next rodeo, and I've been helping him practice."

Megan had never really thought of Ben being any place but the yacht club, a kind of special helper to her and the Tadpoles. Now, in this place, she saw him differently. For a moment or two she watched him as he concentrated on the next event. He looked—well, he looked *right* there: comfortable, relaxed, self-assured.

The rest of the evening was a fascinating, colorful kaleidoscope of sights and sounds. After the rodeo events were over, Ben steered her over to the midway, where the bright lights of the carnival cast a glowing halo against the dark night sky.

"How about it?" Ben asked, stopping in front of the Ferris wheel booth. "Want a ride?"

Megan laughed eagerly, looking up at the spinning circle of lights. "Do you know, I've never been on a Ferris wheel in my life."

"No Ferris wheels?" he asked, buying their tickets. "Next thing you know, you'll be telling me you've never been on a roller coaster, either. You've sure missed out on a lot of things for a rich kid."

"Mom and I aren't rich," Megan answered quickly as they climbed into the swaying car of the Ferris wheel. "And you'd never been in a sailboat until last week. So who's missed out on things?"

"Good point," Ben admitted cheerfully as the attendant latched the bar across their laps and the car started slowly upward. "But if you're not rich, how can you afford a membership at the yacht club?"

"Dad bought a five-year membership for me after he and Mom got divorced. He wanted me to go on sailing. He thought it was a good outdoor sport for me." She swallowed. It was hard for her to talk about the divorce. "Anyway, I guess Dad felt—maybe, a little guilty, like he needed to do something special for me. This was one thing he could do pretty easily without a lot of effort." Megan had decided a long time before that it was better not to talk about her father too much.

"Oh." Ben was silent for a moment. "Well," he added thoughtfully, "I didn't think you were one of *them*."

"Them who?" she asked.

"Them Dolphins," Ben replied with a grin. "Now shut up and enjoy the ride."

At the very top the Ferris wheel paused as another pair of passengers climbed aboard.

Megan shivered. "Cold?" Ben slipped his arm around her shoulders.

"A little." His arm felt warm and comfortable against the back of her neck, and she shivered again, but not from the cold. Almost shyly, she darted a glance at him as the car started to circle swiftly downward. The square line of his jaw made him look proud and mature. His dark brown hair curled softly onto his white collar. He turned and caught Megan looking at him, and he laughed softly.

"Having fun?" he asked lightly. Below, the carnival glimmered like a brightly colored garden, blossoming with lights. Overhead the stars were suspended against the soft black curtain of the sky.

"Oh, yes," Megan said. "This *is* fun." But she couldn't have said whether it was the rodeo and the Ferris wheel or whether it was Ben's nearness that made her feel so good.

When Ben brought Megan home, Mrs. Woods was in the living room working on ledgers for her business. Megan introduced her to Ben and left them to talk while she made a pitcher of iced tea and piled cookies on a plate.

She came back to the living room to find

the two talking comfortably. Mrs. Woods looked up and smiled. "Megan, Ben knows somebody who might be willing to help with the barbecue at the Firecracker Regatta." The previous week, the commodore had called Mrs. Woods to ask if she could handle the food and the serving arrangements for the party after the races. The other caterer had just backed out, so it was very short notice.

Ben smiled at Mrs. Woods. "I have just the girl in mind. She's a hard worker who enjoys being around people, and everybody likes her, too. She's awfully pretty," he added shyly. "I think she'd be a hit with your mother's clients."

"She sounds great. Have her give me a call."

Megan and Ben said good night to Mrs. Woods and took the tea and cookies out to the porch. They sat side by side in the soft darkness on the porch swing. Megan couldn't help thinking about the last time she'd sat there with a boy—Jeff, who had betrayed her so terribly.

"What are you thinking about?" Ben asked gently, reaching for Megan's hand and lightly lacing his fingers into hers.

97

"About the Tadpoles and the Dolphins," Megan said evasively.

"I've been thinking about that a little myself. I've got an idea I think might help both teams."

Megan tensed and tried to pull her hand away, but Ben held it firmly. He turned toward her, and she could see the outline of his face against the light from the window. "It's all right, Megan. Nobody's going to force you to do anything you don't want to do. But I think you should at least listen to my idea."

"Oh, all right," Megan said, her heart thudding heavily.

"I understand that Jeff is expecting a really large turnout for the regatta and that they can't handle all the boats on their small dock. The Tadpoles' dock is very close to the starting line for the races during the regatta. I think you and Jeff might be able to share the Tadpoles' dock."

Megan jerked her hand away angrily. "Did Jeff put you up to this? Did he suggest that you take me out and then come up with this proposition? He ought to know by now that it won't work."

Ben looked at her, his eyes narrowed. "You know better than that, Megan. I don't take orders from Jeff Freeman or from anybody else. But it doesn't take a whole lot to figure out that the Tadpoles' dock is perfect for those extra boats. And it would be great for the Tadpoles to be around the Dolphins and watch how they handle boats. Frankly, I think you and Jeff are acting like a couple of spoiled kids. I don't know what your problem is, but if you two can't solve it, there's going to be a lot of unnecessary confusion—and maybe some accidents—at the regatta."

Megan felt as though her heart were being twisted. It was the same thing, first Jeff, then the commodore, now Ben. And nobody, *nobody* seemed to understand how *she* felt. "There's just not room on the Tadpole dock for the Dolphins," she protested wearily. "All you have to do is look at the space we have and see that we couldn't bring another ten boats onto the dock, much less the seventy-five they expect for the regatta, even though the boats will be using it at different times."

Quietly Ben put his hand on her arm, his fingers strong yet gentle. "Are you going to let me finish telling you my idea?"

"Oh, go on," she said dully.

"We could move the boat racks off the dock onto the shore and build a fifty-foot extension that would give Jeff room to dock the extra boats he expects for the regatta. There'd also be room for you to rig and launch the five boats you're going to use for your sailing demonstration. After the regatta the Dolphins could continue to use the new extension. We'd leave the boat racks on the shore so you'd have enough room to dock all your boats. And some of the Dolphins could give you extra help with the kids, maybe even teach some of the sailing lessons." He paused. "Doesn't that make good sense?"

For a long moment Megan sat still, considering Ben's suggestion. It seemed reasonable. There *was* room to extend the dock. But there was one major problem that had nothing to do with space or convenience or even the commodore's idea of linking the two sailing programs. The real problem wasn't that she wanted to keep the Tadpoles all to herself, as the commodore had suggested. No, the real problem was the way Jeff and the rest of the Dolphins felt about her and the condescending way they talked about the Tadpoles. She frowned and shook her head.

"It won't work, Ben. There are some things that you—that you just don't know about. The Dolphins aren't—well, they're very single-minded about competition. Since I left the team to work with the Tadpoles, they haven't even spoken to me except when Jeff wanted to make a 'deal' with me about the dock." She turned to him. "Don't you see? We just can't work side by side."

Ben leaned forward, elbows on his knees. "I can see that you're having problems with the Dolphins," he said carefully. "And I know that you and Jeff used to be pretty serious about each other. But you can't let your personal feelings get in the way of an arrangement that's in the best interests of both sailing programs, Megan. Maybe you still—like Jeff. I know you feel very hurt. But you need to set those feelings aside and work for the good of both teams." He stood up, pulling her to her feet.

"Megan, I only want what's best for you and the Tadpoles. And in this case, the best thing you can do is settle your differences with Jeff, no matter how hard that is." He put both hands on her shoulders and looked deeply into her eyes. "Please don't say no now. Think about it for a while. And then give Jeff a call and tell him you'd like his help to build the dock extension."

He looked down at her again, and now

there was a different light in his eyes, a light that made Megan's pulse race. She turned away uncertainly. Why was she responding this way? Hadn't she learned her lesson with Jeff? Hadn't she learned to resist being told what to do?

"You're something special, Megan," he said softly and bent and kissed her, his mouth sweet and gentle against hers. Megan's heart was pounding as she relaxed into his arms. The kiss seemed to last forever. For a moment he pulled her head against his shoulder and smoothed her hair. "You're special," he whispered again.

# Chapter Ten

Megan spent the rest of the night and most of the following morning thinking about what Ben had said. "A couple of spoiled kids," he'd called them. She could understand how he might think Jeff was spoiled and childish. After all, he was the one who was behaving so selfishly. But how in the world could he think of her in the same way? She had done the right thing when she accepted the coaching job, hadn't she? The Tadpoles needed her and so did the club. She'd gotten the new program off to a good start, and she was getting fantastic teaching experience. Jeff and the rest of the Dolphins had been so wrong. But then how could Ben call *her* spoiled? It didn't make sense.

It was almost eleven, and she was meeting the Tadpoles at the dock in an hour. Still feeling confused and uncertain, she fixed herself a glass of icy lemonade and went out to sit on the porch swing. The rhododendrons that shaded the front of the porch also filtered the morning breeze, and it felt uncomfortably warm. To the west the sky was darkening, and it looked as if it might storm. The more she tried to put Ben's words out of her mind, the more real they became.

But there was something else bothering her. The memory of Ben's gentle touch, his soft kiss, disturbed her, sweet as it was, because she had no intention of getting involved with him. She admired him, his easy natural way with kids, his skills, his self-confidence. But the two of them were so different. He wasn't like anyone she had ever known, and that difference made her feel nervous. It was as though being with him made her question everything she'd done in the past year—spending so much time racing with the Dolphins, not meeting other kids with other interests and, most recently, keeping the Tadpoles separate from the Dolphins. She frowned and pushed the swing. What was it about Ben that made her feel this way? "A couple of spoiled kids," she heard again, and after a minute she sighed and went to the telephone.

Hearing Jeff's voice, once so warm and caring, was very painful, and she swallowed hard. "Jeff, I need to talk to you. Got a minute?"

"Sure," he said and yawned. He sounded as though he'd just gotten up. "What's going on?"

"I've been thinking about the dock situation for the regatta." There was no point in telling him about Ben's part in this; it would just make him uncomfortable. "I guess you guys really are crowded at the Dolphin dock, and I think we might be able to work something out."

"Oh yeah?" Jeff's voice was enthusiastic but guarded, as though he didn't really trust her.

"We could move the dinghy racks off the Tadpole dock and build an extension next to the launch area. That would probably give you enough dock space." She took a deep breath. "What do you think?"

There was a long silence and then Jeff said quietly, "Megan, I don't know how to thank you. You're really helping us out of a bad spot. I'm going to make sure that the rest of the gang knows whose idea this was." There was a smile in his voice, and Megan heard some of the old warmth. "It'll change their minds about a lot of things."

Megan tried to make her voice light and casual, but Jeff's words reminded her of how much she used to care for him—still cared. She clutched the receiver tightly. "Of course, there's a catch to it," she said as brightly as she could. "How are your carpentry skills? We've got a lot of building to do, and just a little over a week before the regatta."

"I'll get the gang together and meet you out at the lake in an hour," he said promptly. "Wait till you see how good we are at dock building!"

By the time she got out to the lake they were all there, talking together, pointing out where the new dock should be built and where the boat racks could be relocated. Several of the team members seemed to have decided already what to do when Jeff held up his hand for silence.

"Wait a minute," he said. "This is the Tadpoles' dock, and we're the invited guests, so everybody just settle down. Megan, what do we do first?" With a smile that made her heart tumble, he drew Megan into the group.

"Before we start anything," she said carefully, "we have to check with the commodore and see whether he has any objections. And then we'll have to ask Ben to help us draw up the plans for the renovation since he's in charge of all renovations for the Tadpoles."

"Ben?" Jeff asked quickly.

Gary nudged him with a sly smile. "You know, the guy with the cowboy hat."

Jeff nodded. "Well, I guess we'll need some help to get the job done. Doesn't matter who gives it to us."

Megan glanced around the group. They were listening intently and trading pleased grins. Megan felt a wonderful glow of triumph, and she turned to smile at Jeff. "I'm glad we could work out a way to bring the two teams closer together."

Megan asked Mindy and Gary to meet with the Tadpoles so she could go with Jeff to meet the commodore in his office. They went to the deck overlooking the lake to explain what they planned to do. "We'll move the boat racks over there by the mesquite tree," Megan pointed out, "and then extend the dock about fifty feet along the shore. That should give us all room to work during the regatta."

"And afterward?" the commodore asked.

Jeff looked at Megan. "We'd like to continue to dock there sometimes," he said eagerly. "That is, if Megan thinks that's all right for the Tadpoles."

"If the arrangement works out during the regatta, I guess we'd have no objection."

"Good!" the commodore exclaimed. "Now, why don't you two sit down with Ben and draw up some sketches before you begin? The Tadpoles look like they're in good hands down there. And remember that we want a good job, not just something you throw together in an afternoon."

"No, sir," Jeff promised. "You can bet we'll do a first-rate job."

They found Ben working at the boat repair shed, and Megan couldn't help but notice again the sharp contrast between him and Jeff. Ben was wearing his old blue jeans, faded and patched at the knee, and a paint-stained white T-shirt. Little rivulets of sweat were running down his dusty face. Jeff, on the other hand, was wearing a pair of crisp white sailing shorts with a smart red stripe down either side and a bright red T-shirt. Next to him Ben looked grimy, disheveled, and just a little ordinary.

But Ben's grin was friendly. "Finally got your act together?" he asked teasingly.

Jeff put his arm around Megan's shoulders and hugged her briefly. "Looks like we're on the right track," he said, smiling down at her. "Teamwork all the way."

Uneasily Megan avoided Ben's direct gaze. It hadn't been honest to take credit for the plan. "A—a lot of this was Ben's idea," she muttered. "He's the one who suggested adding an extension to the dock."

Puzzled, Jeff looked from one to the other. "Well, it really doesn't matter whose idea it was," he said at last. "But now we really need to get going. Ben, let's see if we can draw up a plan and figure out what we'll have to buy."

The rest of the afternoon was spent planning, measuring, drawing, and then redrawing until everyone was satisfied with the proposed dock extension. The commodore approved the plans, and Ben and Jeff drove to the lumberyard to buy supplies.

After that the work went smoothly. Ben showed everyone how to treat the wooden posts that would support the dock and how to prepare cardboard molds for concrete bases.

"I'll rent a small concrete mixer tomorrow," he told them, "and we'll mix the concrete and pour it into the molds. Then after it sets, we can sink the concrete bases into the lake and begin framing the dock itself."

"But what can we do in the meantime?" Gary demanded impatiently. "Time's getting short. The regatta's going to be here before the dock is finished—"

Ben shook his head. "No problem, Gary. It'll be a big job, but we'll make it. And there's plenty to do before we begin building. While we're working on these forms, why don't you take a crew and start moving the boat racks?"

The next few days were incredibly busy. Jeff picked Megan up every morning at eight, and she helped the Dolphins work on the dock until noon. Megan had scheduled extra practice sessions for the Tadpoles so their exhibition would be perfect. She had them come at one. About four, when the last of the kids went home, the Dolphins were usually just finishing their own sailing practice, and Jeff would drive Megan home.

At first Megan felt uncomfortable because of everything that had happened between her and Jeff. But their relationship quickly slipped into the old pattern she remembered so well. He began driving her home every evening. On Wednesday evening as she was about to get out of the car, Jeff reached for her hand. "I'm glad it's worked out this way, Megan," he said softly. "You were right to stay on with the Tadpoles. And your idea of building the dock extension is terrific. Now, can we forget what happened and get on with it—together?"

*Together!* Megan's heart leapt with joy. He wanted the two of them to be a couple again. Now she had everything—Jeff, her work, and a new friendship with the others on the team. But something nagged at her, something that reminded her Ben was an important part of her life now. But she put it out of her mind. She'd wanted Jeff for a long time, and now she could have him.

"Yes, let's get on with it, Jeff," she said softly.

Jeff pulled her against him for a long, tender kiss that made Megan feel weak. "How about a movie tomorrow night?" His warm lips brushed her ear, and a shiver ran down her back.

Megan pulled away and looked up at him. "Of course," she answered joyfully. "Oh, Jeff,

I'm so glad we've gotten back together again." And as she ran into the house, she felt as though she were flying, she was so happy.

On Thursday they finished the extension, and the Dolphins decided to skip practice and go swimming at Paleface Park. Megan couldn't go because the Tadpoles had afternoon practice. Things hadn't gone too well, and by the time all the kids left, Megan felt exhausted.

Still, it was a lovely summer evening, and the sunlight slanted in gold rays across the water. As Megan stood alone on the new dock, she felt as though she hadn't been by herself in weeks. The silence and the aloneness felt good. Since she had started dating Jeff again, her evenings were filled, and the days were so busy she didn't have time to think about anything except finishing the dock project and getting the Tadpoles ready for their exhibition.

A shadow fell across her feet, and she looked up. It was Ben, a fishing rod in his hand, his black cowboy hat tipped back on his head. He squatted on his heels beside her and looked out across the lake.

"Peaceful, isn't it," he said after a long, calm silence.

Megan sighed. "I love the evening hours out here."

"But you're not spending them here, are you?" Ben asked. He tied on a small yellow lure and flicked it smoothly into the water.

Megan sneaked a glance at him. He looked more mature than the boys she knew. She remembered his kiss and the warmth of his arms. She looked away and shivered. That was just—just an interlude while she was waiting for Jeff to come back to her. She might have been temporarily attracted to Ben, but her heart belonged to Jeff.

"No," she said slowly, "I've been spending a lot of time with the Dolphins."

He twitched his line. "Isn't it Jeff who's taking up your evenings?"

"Yes," she said again. And then, after a minute or two, she added, "I know that none of this would have happened without you. It was your idea to build the dock extension, and that was what made the rest of these things happen. I—I want to say thank you."

"I don't need any thanks," he said gruffly, not looking at her, "unless you're inclined to go to the rodeo with me tonight. There's something special I'd like you to see."

"Oh, I'm sorry, Ben," she said regretfully. "I've already made other plans." Funny, she really was sorry. Being with Ben would have been fun.

Suddenly Ben's rod tip bent, and he reeled in the line quickly. "Sorry about tonight," he said, not looking at her. "But as long as you've got what you want, as long as you're happy, that's good enough for me." The hook dangled emptily as he pulled it in, and Ben sighed.

"Missed again," he said simply and stood up. "Let me know if I can help with the regatta on Saturday," he added, still not looking at her, and walked away.

Later that night, when she and Jeff walked into Maxwell's after the movie, the whole team was there crowded around the corner table, their usual spot. They moved over to make room for Jeff and Megan.

"Been to the movies?" Gary asked.

Jeff nodded. "Just a usual Thursday night," he said, winking at Megan. It was a wink that told the others they had something special going between them.

Mindy looked up brightly. "Gary and I

114

decided *not* to do the usual tonight," she said, making a face. "The usual gets so boring."

"What did you do?" Megan asked politely. Since she and Jeff had gotten back together, Mindy was dating Gary again.

"We went to the Caldwell County Rodeo," Mindy said. "And guess who we saw there?"

"Who?" Jeff asked curiously, gesturing to the waitress. "Two chocolate sundaes with the works, please."

"Megan's old friend Ben was the star of the cowboy opera tonight," she said smugly. "He won the bucking bronco contest."

"Really?" Jeff asked with interest. "I didn't know Ben was into horses." He turned to Megan. "Did you?"

Megan thought with a flash of pleasure of the evening they had spent together at the rodeo. "Yes, I knew," she said simply. She turned to Mindy. "Did he—did he get thrown off?"

Mindy shrugged carelessly. "Nope. He stayed on longer than anybody else. Looked like he had an easy horse. And for once, his cowboy hat looked right at home."

Gary laughed. "That horse only looked easy because Ben was so good. It was a great

115

change of pace," he said, turning to Jeff. "We ought to do things like that more often, instead of spending so much of our time at the lake."

"Sure, sure," Jeff said impatiently. "Now let's talk about the regatta. Louise tells me we've got a problem with the registrations. Here's what I think we ought to do. . . ."

And for the rest of the evening, Jeff and Gary talked about plans for the regatta while Mindy chattered away about her newly married cousin in Houston. But Megan wasn't listening. All the while she was imagining the rodeo and a boy in a black cowboy hat, his arm flung high in the air, astride a bucking mare.

# Chapter Eleven

Saturday dawned beautifully clear with a fair, brisk wind. The weather couldn't have been more perfect for the regatta. Excitedly Megan got up early, anxious to get out to the lake and make sure everything was set for the Tadpoles' sailing exhibition. Before the kids got there, she would have to check all the gear and lay it out neatly. There'd be enough confusion even if everything was right where it should be. Misplaced equipment could mean disaster.

At eight Jeff pulled up in the drive and honked his horn. "Ready?" he yelled. The backseat of his car was filled with extra life jackets and spare sets of sails.

Megan opened her window. "In a minute," she called. Hurriedly she pulled the brush through her gleaming hair once more and looked approvingly at herself in the mirror. The out-of-doors work she'd been doing all summer had given her a glowing, healthy tan and lightened her dark blond hair. And she'd been sailing so much and working so hard, she'd lost almost five pounds. Even to her own eyes she looked better than middling these days.

Mrs. Woods was up early, too, handling the last-minute details for the barbeque. She was at the kitchen table, checking over a long list. "Daisies," she muttered. "And aprons for the helpers, two extra boxes of plastic trash bags—" She broke off and looked up as Megan dashed through the kitchen door.

"You look extra nice this morning," she said approvingly. "All set for the big day?"

"All set," Megan said happily, grabbing two doughnuts from the box on the counter. "How about you?"

"I certainly hope so," her mother said, then laughed. "But there'll be something I've forgotten. There always is, especially with a job this big." She turned to Megan. "I suppose you'll be too busy with Jeff and Company to give us a hand."

Megan frowned. "Are you shorthanded tonight?" She had worked so hard getting ready for that day, and she'd planned to relax and enjoy the party with Jeff and the others.

Mrs. Woods waved her hand. "No, dear. I'm sure we can do without you. But do stop by and say hello," she added. "I'll be the one with the big knife, slicing the barbequed beef."

Megan laughed and gave her mother a brief hug. "OK, see you tonight, Mom."

Jeff was waiting impatiently beside the car. "I was about ready to come in and carry you out," he said, joking, but his voice had a little edge to it. "We're going to be late."

"Sorry," Megan said, handing him one of the doughnuts. "I stopped to talk to Mom. You know she's handling the barbeque tonight, and that's a pretty big job."

Jeff looked at her in alarm as he turned the key in the ignition. "You don't have to help her tonight, do you? I thought we'd have the evening together, cut out early before the presentations, take a few of the gang, and go to a movie over in Centerville."

"But, Jeff, you know I can't miss the

presentations," Megan protested. "We're handing out the Tadpoles' certificates, and I have to be there for that. Anyway," she coaxed, "won't you have to be there to handle first-day winners' presentations?"

"I guess so," he said reluctantly. He looked at her again, his eyes growing warm. "Hey, you look terrific. Going anyplace special?"

"Silly." Megan slapped his arm playfully and settled back into the seat. It was going to be a great day, and she could hardly wait to get to work.

By noon the kids had arrived to get ready for their sailing demonstration. Each one had a special responsibility, something to arrange for the exhibition. But that didn't lighten Megan's work load because she still had to oversee all the different projects. Three of the kids were kneeling on the dock cutting pennants from colored vinyl strips, and two others were fastening them to the masthead rigging of the boats. Several others were in the cove in a rowboat setting the exhibition course by mooring buoys at specific points. Still another group had set up the Tadpoles' cookie and lemonade booth on the clubhouse patio—the Great Cookie Caper, one of the kids had nicknamed it—and it was already doing a brisk business as the day grew warmer.

Megan was supervising the group setting the course by shouting directions through a megaphone from the shore. At the same time, she was keeping an eye on the pennant cutters. One little boy was waving a pair of scissors around and threatening to give Pam a haircut. At just that moment Sam ran down from the patio and announced that they needed more change at the cookie booth—immediately.

Megan sighed. The regatta had only just begun, and she was exhausted already. Still, she thought, no matter what happened at the sailing exhibition, the hard work and the long hours had all been worth it. She watched the Tadpoles working with skill, concentration, and confidence. Ben was right. The important thing about teaching wasn't what the kids learned to do, it was how they learned to feel about themselves. And judging from these noisy, productive, busy kids, her teaching had been successful.

On the new dock the Dolphins were also busy. The small-boat turnout had been even bigger than they'd expected. "Looks like we'll have about eighty boats out here this weekend," Gary told Jeff with concern in his voice. "It's a darn good thing they all race in different classes. We couldn't handle all of them at once."

But even so, the boat traffic was heavy in the cove, and Megan was concerned about the safety of the kids in the rowboat. "Hey, Tod, finish up in a hurry and bring the boat back in, will you?" she called. The rowboat was difficult to turn, and if a fast boat came up quickly, there could be a bad accident.

By two o'clock, the time the Tadpoles' sailing exhibition was scheduled, the whole cove was in mad confusion. The larger Santanas and the Thistles were rigging up on the far side, out of the way. But some of the skippers didn't seem to pay any attention to the exhibition markers and took shortcuts through the course the Tadpoles had laid out. And the Dolphins weren't much help, either. They had their hands full getting boats rigged and into the water. And their area was so crowded that people were beginning to spill over onto the Tadpole dock.

Finally, in desperation, Megan pulled Jeff aside. "I need some help here, Jeff," she pleaded. "There's so much confusion, I'm afraid somebody's going to get hurt. And now that the first finishers are starting to pull in, there's no room to get our dinghies rigged for the exhibition. You're going to have to get some of these boats out of here so we can get started."

Jeff looked hot and cross. "It's perfectly obvious that we've got a problem, Megan," he said, scowling. "You'll just have to tough it out until we can get these boats away from here."

"But we would've been OK if it weren't for you guys," she said pointedly, trying to keep the frustrated annoyance out of her voice. "The least you could do is tell the incoming boats to move closer together and give us enough room to get the dinghies in the water."

"Look, Megan," Jeff said brusquely, "the next race is more important than your exhibition. I'll be glad to help you when we're finished with this bunch."

"Sorry, that's not good enough. Can't you just move those Fireballs closer together?"

Jeff stared at her for a moment. "OK, OK," he said grudgingly, turning away. "I'll see what I can do. But I can't promise anything."

Jeff's hurried instructions to Gary and Louise improved things a little, but Megan could see that they still weren't going to be able to launch the dinghies from the dock anytime in the next half hour. She glanced nervously at her watch. The kids were waiting impatiently, already wearing their life jackets and grouped according to their boat assignments. Nearly two dozen spectators, mostly parents and club members, were lined up on the patio and the deck with binoculars, waiting for the exhibition to begin. But unless Jeff cleared some of the boats away, it looked as if the exhibition might not get started at all.

"Got a problem?"

Megan turned quickly, pushing the damp hair out of her eyes. It was Ben, looking composed and self-possessed, and she felt a great surge of relief when she saw him. "Well, yes, as a matter of fact, we have a *big* problem," she said, taking a deep breath to steady herself. "The Dolphins seem to have taken over the entire dock area, in spite of our agreement. And they aren't helping me one bit, the way they said they would."

"OK, settle down," Ben said quietly. "There's nothing here that we can't handle with a little imagination. Now, why don't we use the old launching area to get the boats in the water? It'll just take a minute longer, and kids can carry the dinghies from the rack to the launch area just as easily as they can carry them to the dock."

Megan considered. "But Jeff agreed—" she began again.

Ben gripped her arm firmly. "Look, Megan," he said steadily, "Jeff has more than he can manage at the moment, and the agreements you're talking about don't mean a heck of a lot right now. It's more practical for you to find another solution than to hold Jeff to a bargain he can't possibly keep. So let's see if we can work something out."

Ben's solution was a success, and in fifteen minutes the entire Tadpole fleet was in the water, pennants flying gaily. Tod and Megan had arranged the course so that the kids could demonstrate their ability to handle everything. They ran tacks and jibes, racing starts, and sail changes, using colorful little spinnakers. And they topped it all off with their favorite man-overboard drill, in which half the crew splashed noisily in the water and the skippers had to execute several tricky, perfectly timed maneuvers to pick them up.

From the shore Megan called out instructions with her megaphone. It was a great exhibition. Several times, she looked toward the Dolphins' dock, hoping that Jeff was watching, too, but he was always deep in conversation with someone.

When the exhibition was over, it was a little harder to get the boats up the old launching ramp, but Ben was there to help, wading up to his waist to help the kids.

Tod's boat was the first one in. "Didn't we do good, Megan?" he called excitedly. "Did you see us get the spinnaker up without twisting it?"

Megan smiled happily. "Sure thing, Tod. Everybody did a terrific job."

When the boats were all on the shore, Ben turned to Megan. "Congratulations, teacher," he said, grinning, "you did one fantastic job." He shook his head in mock amazement. "Three weeks ago I wouldn't have given a plugged nickel for your chances of turning this wild bunch into sailors."

Megan blushed with pleasure. "Thanks, Ben," she murmured. She glanced again in Jeff's direction, but he was still preoccupied with the latest group of arrivals and didn't look up.

In an hour, with Ben lending a hand, all

the sails were packed, and the boats were stowed on the racks. Megan hurried off to see how the Great Cookie Caper was coming along. The sailing exhibition had been a tremendous success.

But, somehow, Megan wasn't as happy as she'd expected to be. She felt restless and a bit unsatisfied as she helped the kids at the booth set out trays of cookies and make more lemonade. What in the world was the matter with her? She had just seen all her hard work pay off, hadn't she? The exhibition had gone very well, in spite of the initial problems. Just as important, the Dolphins were now *her* friends, not just Jeff's, since she'd been the one to arrange for their new dock. She wouldn't have to worry about losing their friendship or being snubbed by them. And most important of all, she and Jeff were again together—even though she wished he'd been a little more cooperative during the exhibition.

Thanks heavens Ben had been there, just as he always was. For a moment she stood still, stunned. *Ben* was the one she'd depended on to get things done. It had been his generosity, his helpfulness, and above all, his belief in her that had helped to pull it all together. Jeff had given her nothing but orders and extra problems. Suddenly she realized it was Ben she admired, not Jeff.

"Hey, Megan," Sam cried, "we need more cookies again." And for the rest of the afternoon, Megan was too busy to think about anything.

# Chapter Twelve

By six o'clock most of the sailors had docked their boats, finished their clean-up chores, and started to gather on the clubhouse patio, sunburned and tired, to talk over the events of the day. Mrs. Woods's catering crew had set up a dozen trestle tables on the lawn, covered with cheerful red-checked tablecloths and decorated with wicker baskets of white daisies and ferns. Dozens of colorful Japanese lanterns were strung between the trees. The serving tables were lined up beside the tennis courts and loaded with spicy barbequed beef, pork ribs, plump sausages, steaming vats of baked beans cooked in rich tomato sauce, and trays heaped high with hot ears of sweet corn.

After she and the kids had dismantled the Great Cookie Caper stand, Megan stood off to the side watching her mother's crew take care of the last-minute details.

She remembered how embarrassed she had been about her mother's catering business, and she felt a quick, hot flash of shame. How had she let herself become so conceited, so narrow-minded, and unfair? After a moment she shook her head and went off to find her mother in the clubhouse kitchen.

"Well, hello, my dear," Mrs. Woods said, looking up from a kettle of bubbling barbeque sauce. The sweet, pungent smell of tomato sauce and hickory-smoked meat hung in the warm air. The kitchen was crowded with helpers, each working smoothly, knowing exactly what to do. "I hear that your sailing exhibition this afternoon was a smashing success."

"Yes, it was," Megan said composedly. "And if it hadn't been for Ben's good sense and quick thinking, it might have *really* been smashing. With all the boats at the Dolphins' end of the dock, we had a real traffic jam. We were lucky there weren't any collisions. But in spite of the confusion, it was fun, and the kids felt very good about it—and themselves." She glanced around the busy kitchen. "Now, where's my apron? I'm here to help."

"Your apron? But, Megan, you don't have to help tonight. You must be tired, and you've earned a rest. We're a little shorthanded because Mike didn't show up, but—"

"No, Mom, you don't understand. I know I don't have to help, but I want to, anyway." She smiled warmly and put her arm around her mother's shoulders. "Really I do."

Mrs. Woods put down her spoon, and Megan knew it wasn't going to be as easy as she'd hoped. "Have you and Jeff had a falling out?" her mother asked, her gray eyes warm and direct.

Megan looked away. Much as she loved her mother, she didn't want to share her feelings right then. Later, maybe, when she'd sorted them out, but not just then. "No, no fight," she said honestly, meeting her mother's eyes. "I just don't feel like spending the whole evening with Jeff and the gang, and I thought I could help with the serving. After dinner I have to give the commodore a hand with the certificate presentations, but later I'd be glad to work on cleanup."

"Well, I've never been one to turn away anybody who came looking for work," her mother said cheerfully, handing her an old-fashioned, red-checked apron. "Welcome aboard. Here's something to keep you clean, and there's a big bowl of potato salad that belongs on the table outside. Then ask Mattie to show you what to do."

Mattie was putting the final touches on the serving table. She was strikingly pretty with ebony black hair and large, dark brown eyes rimmed with thick black lashes. Her hair was tied back with a blue scarf, and her aqua shirt and checked apron set off her deeply tanned skin. *So, this is Ben's friend,* Megan thought with a pang of envy. *No wonder he spoke about her with such pride. She's one of the prettiest girls I've ever seen.*

When Megan introduced herself, Mattie smiled. She had a bright and friendly smile that created deep dimples at the corners of her mouth. "Something to do?" she said in response to Megan's question. "Sure, there's lots. Why don't you put the salt and pepper shakers on the tables over there and then grab a pitcher from Hank so you can help fill all those empty glasses with iced tea. By that time everybody will be lined up for dinner, and you can help dish up the beans."

Megan had just poured the last glass of iced tea and was getting ready to take up her station behind the huge cast-iron bean pot when Jeff caught her. "Hey, what's this?" he asked, wrinkling up his nose in distaste and tugging on the string of her gingham apron. "You said you didn't have to work with the kitchen crew. I thought we were ready for some real fun."

Steadying herself, Megan gave him a long, appraising look. She had been hearing that commanding tone in his voice ever since the first day they'd met, but somehow it had never really registered. Why had she been so deaf? But that night was a new beginning, and she knew what she had to do. "Sorry, Jeff," she said confidently, "I told Mom I'd give her a hand with the serving and the cleanup, and after dinner I have to help the commodore with the Tadpole presentations. Why don't you go on and eat with the others?"

Jeff put his hand on her arm. "I'm confused," he said incredulously. "Is there something going on around here that I don't understand?"

Megan shook her head. "No, nothing's

going on, really. I—I just want to help Mom."
She took a deep breath. "Let's talk later."

"But I thought we had a date tonight,"
Jeff persisted.

Megan looked at him. "We did," she said
flatly. "But I've decided to work."

"Well, OK," Jeff said reluctantly, still dis-
believing, "if you're sure this is what you want
to do. I'll call you tomorrow. OK?"

Megan nodded. "OK," she said quietly.

"Hey, skipper," Mindy called, waving jaun-
tily at Jeff, "we're already in line. Come on,
you don't want to miss the barbeque!" And
Jeff turned away to join the rest of the
Dolphins.

By the time everyone had eaten all the
barbequed beef, beans, and corn they could
hold, the sun was beginning to blaze its way
through the cedar trees on the hills to the
west, and the evening breeze was picking up
a sweet, fragrant coolness from the lake. The
commodore gathered the group into the assembly hall to announce the names of the
winners for the day. Megan rounded up the
Tadpoles, and they all sat together on the floor
in front of the hall.

The commodore stood up and motioned for silence. "The regatta's off to a great start, folks, thanks to everyone who has worked so hard for the past few weeks. There's more racing tomorrow, of course, but tonight we're going to announce first-day scores and check off the names of all the top finishers, just to be sure there's no mix-up." He glanced down at the twins, Pam and Sam, who were squirming impatiently, practically under his feet.

"But before we get started with the main part of the evening, I'd like to introduce a very special bunch of kids, our Tadpoles. These kids have spent a lot of hours learning to sail, and this afternoon they put on a remarkable demonstration of their skills. Now I want you to meet these hardworking kids and their coach, Megan Woods."

"OK, gang, here we go," Megan whispered. The Tadpoles pushed and jostled one another noisily as they stood up. The commodore read out the names of the youngsters who had completed the new program and handed out engraved certificates. Megan gave a special hug to each one. It had been a tough job, but every minute of it had paid off. Megan watched as each child accepted his or her certificate proudly. A deep satisfaction filled her with happiness.

When the certificates had been distributed and Megan had the kids sitting down again, the commodore motioned for her to remain standing at the front. "Hang on just a little bit, Megan," he said. "I want to tell everyone more about the program and about your contributions to it." Megan listened, glowing with pride and a bit of embarrassment, as the commodore described the Tadpole sailing program and Megan's development of it. "Now, thanks to Megan Woods," he concluded with satisfaction, "we have a junior sailing team to match our senior sailing team—and a great new dock that both teams can share. Megan, we're all proud of what you've accomplished, and we have a certificate for you, too."

Blushing with pleasure, Megan stepped forward to the applause of the crowd. And then, at the back of the room, Megan saw Ben. He was leaning comfortably against the wall, wearing his dusty old cowboy hat, and as he caught her eye, he flashed her a delighted grin and a thumbs-up sign. Standing next to him, looking up at him with a great deal of obvious admiration, was his friend Mattie.

Both dark-skinned and dark-haired, both very attractive, they looked as though they belonged together.

At that moment Megan remembered how she'd felt after the exhibition. She realized then that a lot of the credit for what she and the Tadpoles had achieved over the past few weeks didn't really belong to her—but to Ben. It was Ben who had urged her to settle her differences with Jeff and the Dolphins, and it was Ben who had recommended that they build the new dock. And it was *that* suggestion, strangely enough, that had brought a sudden end to their warm and caring relationship because the dock project had brought her and Jeff together again and made her a Dolphin once more. She straightened her shoulders. It was OK to keep her friendship with the Dolphins. But it *wasn't* OK to be trapped within their narrow perimeters. And it *wasn't* OK to take credit for Ben's work.

"Thank you," she said as she shook the commodore's hand. Funny, she wasn't at all nervous, the way she usually was when she had to speak to a group. She faced the crowd and raised her voice firmly. "Thanks for your support and help," she said. "This hasn't been the kind of project that anybody can carry out alone, and I need to thank the commodore, for having confidence in me, and Mr. Conrad and several others for leading some wonderful discussions with the kids." She caught Ben's gaze, then looked away quickly. For an instant she couldn't bear to look at him. She lifted her chin and took a deep breath.

"But the person we really ought to thank for all the progress the Tadpoles have made this year is Ben Holliday, who managed all of the repair and construction work. It was Ben's idea to build the dock extension, and it was his everyday help that made the Tadpoles' exhibition possible today." Now she could look at him.

And as Ben smiled at the loud applause, Megan knew for certain that he was the one she really cared about. Jeff still had a lot of growing up to do.

Megan felt sad that she'd spoiled her chance with Ben, the chance for something *special.* She hoped only that they could work out any bad feelings she'd caused by her selfish behavior and continue to be friends.

Ben grinned crookedly at Megan. Suddenly she was exhausted. And as she sank back in her seat, she knew it wasn't weariness that made her want to cry or tiredness that made her shoulders sag. It was sadness, the sadness that comes with the acknowledgment of real loss. What she had lost was Ben. And Jeff was only a poor substitute.

# Chapter Thirteen

For the next few days Megan felt a tremendous letdown after the frantic activity of the previous weeks. To give herself some breathing room, she hadn't scheduled the next Tadpole group to begin for another week, and even the Dolphins were taking a short vacation from sailing.

At first Megan welcomed the break in the hectic routine. She slept until almost eleven and spent most of the day doing things she'd put off—making a new blouse and a ruffled prairie skirt and cleaning her room. It was exactly the kind of pleasant, relaxing time she'd been missing all summer long.

But Megan couldn't really enjoy her freedom; she found herself restless and on edge. Everything had changed for her. For many months Jeff had been the center of her life. Even during the time they'd separated because of the Tadpoles, she had wanted to be with him, and the day he'd come back had been the happiest one of her life.

But she knew that their relationship was over now. He had called the day after the regatta to remind her of their plans to go to the boat show. But Megan found herself making an excuse not to go.

"Hey, I don't understand what's going on," Jeff said with genuine puzzlement in his voice. "Saturday night after the regatta you were really acting funny, but I decided that it was because you were tired from the work and frustrated because of all the problems. But everything ought to be back on track now. What gives?"

Megan sighed. There really wasn't any easy way to do this. She would just have to tell him. Taking a deep breath, she squared her shoulders and said, "I don't think we should see each other anymore, Jeff. I've decided that—that I need something different, something we don't have together."

There was a stunned silence on the other end of the line. "You're sure?" Jeff said finally.

Megan twisted the cord around her fingers. "I'm sure," she whispered.

"Well, I'm sure not going to beg," Jeff said coldly. "If that's the way you want it, that's the way you've got it. See you around."

And that was that. Funny how something you wanted so badly could turn out to be so wrong, she reflected, as she put down the telephone. But the knowledge didn't bring her any comfort. It wasn't this final breakup with Jeff that made her feel so empty, so alone, it was knowing that she had lost Ben. *That* was the thing that hurt her the most, that twisted inside her every time she thought about it.

Her mother seemed to know how Megan was feeling and tried to cheer her up. "I really appreciated your help the other night with the barbecue," she said warmly when Megan came into the kitchen to fix herself some lunch. "Did you enjoy working with the crew?"

Megan put down the lemonade pitcher and considered. "Well, yes, I guess I did," she said honestly. "I hadn't intended to, but I did."

Her mother looked up from the pile of

bills she was working on. "If that's true, then maybe you'd like to help with the picnic we're putting together on Saturday for a family reunion down on the river," she said, then added hastily, "I'm only suggesting, mind you. Things are going along pretty well. But I'll need somebody to help me load up the van with all the sandwiches and things. You can unload at the park and then do whatever you like."

Buttering her bread, Megan said thoughtfully, "I'd like to help. I need to do something different for a change, and I don't have any responsibilities at the lake this weekend. I guess I've spent too much time at the club since we moved here. I don't seem to know very much about the rest of Texas or to have any friends outside the kids I know from sailing." She looked up and smiled weakly. "Seems to me I remember somebody—maybe my mother—saying something like that a while ago."

Mrs. Woods nodded cheerfully. "Well, something like that, anyway. But now that things are a little more relaxed, maybe you'll have time to find some different activities. And when you go back to the Tadpoles next week, perhaps you can involve some different people in your plans and make some new friends."

"I will," Megan said firmly, but in spite of her conviction, she felt at a loss. It was easy to *say* that she'd make new friends, but a lot harder to do it. And while she really meant what she said about taking part in new activities, it was awfully hard to do all by herself.

That Saturday Megan helped her mother load the van with the picnic food and supplies. They worked quietly for a couple of hours that afternoon, and Megan felt a deep satisfaction in their ability to work so well together. She hadn't thought of it that way, but she and her mother were a good team.

"OK, I guess that's it," Mrs. Woods said as they loaded the last box. "Why don't you drive the van to the park, and I'll come along in a few minutes. The crew is down there already. Mattie is helping set things up. Look for the signs along the road."

The picnic was taking place at the far end of the park along the river. Megan followed the signs pointing in the direction of the picnic area. She could see a large group of children and adults already gathered along the green banks, playing badminton, horse-shoes, and Frisbee. A few people were even fishing. After a minute she located Mattie.

"Hi! I thought maybe you'd gotten lost," Mattie said as they opened the van doors and began to carry the boxes of food to the work-tables.

"Your signs were a big help," Megan said. "Some of those turns are really confusing."

"You ought to find Ben and tell him," Mattie answered. "He made them. Anyway, he's been looking for you."

"For me?" Megan's heart turned over. "Is he here this afternoon?"

"Yes, he brought me over. But I think he really wanted to see you," Mattie said with a smile.

Megan looked confused. "Well, OK," she said slowly. Why was Mattie saying something like that to her? And did Ben really want to see her? Guardedly, she asked, "Where did you see him last?"

Mattie pointed in the direction of the river. "He was headed that way with Dog and his fishing gear. I can get someone else to help me unload the rest of the stuff. Why don't you go find him?"

Megan nodded, even more confused, but

she set off in the direction that Mattie pointed. In a few minutes she found Ben squatting easily on his heels, his hat cocked back, intent on the fishing rod he held lightly.

Megan approached him uneasily. "OK if I sit down for a minute?" she asked.

Ben swiveled around, his face breaking into a wide grin. "I hoped you'd come," he said happily. "I heard you were going to help out this afternoon."

Megan brushed aside some leaves and twigs and sat down. "Yes, I helped Mom load the van. I saw your signs. They're really neat." She avoided looking at him.

"Thanks. I thought they might help." He glanced sideways at her. "How are things with you?"

Megan reached for a small stick lying nearby and began nervously peeling its bark off. "OK," she said slowly. Should she say anything about breaking up with Jeff?

"I also heard that you and Jeff aren't seeing each other," he said, almost as if he'd read her mind. He reeled in his line and flicked it into the water again.

Megan looked out across the quiet, still water, watching the ripples widen slowly where Ben's lure had disappeared. "Yes, that's right.

I decided that I needed to—to get a little different perspective on things."

"Are you sad?"

"No, I don't think so. It's just that—" She couldn't tell him how she really felt, that the emptiness inside her grew out of a realization that *he* was the one she cared for. "It's just that I'd sort of put all my eggs in one basket," she said lamely, turning her face away. "And now I have to find some different friends and some new things to do."

Ben stood up quickly and reeled in his line. "New things to do, huh? You've given me the perfect lead-in, Megan," he said with satisfaction. He whistled for Dog, who came bounding through the underbrush along the bank. "Come on, we're on our way."

Megan laughed. Why was Ben always so impulsive? "But I don't understand," she said, climbing to her feet. "On our way where?"

"To get a different perspective on things," Ben said mysteriously, pulling her along. Quickly they made their way back to the picnic area, where Mattie and Mrs. Woods were deep in conversation.

"Mrs. Woods, if you're finished with Megan, I'd like to kidnap her for a couple of hours," Ben said. "OK?"

Megan's mother looked up from the list she held in her hand. "Thanks for helping with the loading, Megan. Sure, go ahead."

Mattie turned to Ben. "Tell Mom that Karen is giving me a lift home," she said. "It'll probably be late."

"OK, sis."

Megan nearly stopped breathing. Sis? Was Mattie Ben's *sister*? So that was why they seemed so natural together! And why she looked at him so admiringly the night of the regatta. As they climbed into the truck, she said as casually as she could, "I didn't realize Mattie was your sister."

"What? Well, I guess it just never got mentioned while you were around," Ben said, turning on the key. "Who did you think she was?"

Megan turned to look out the window. "Well, I guess I—I thought she was your girlfriend," she confessed.

Ben threw back his head and laughed as he shifted gears, and behind them, in the back of the truck, Dog barked at an imaginary rabbit beside the road. "Sorry for laughing like that," he said finally, "but I'm complimented. My little sister's a really pretty girl. It makes me feel good to hear that you thought she'd go for me."

They rode in silence for a time, down a twisting gravel road lined with juniper and gnarled oak trees, through part of the countryside Megan had never seen before. At the end of the road, they came into a clearing with a neat white stucco ranchhouse at one end and a cluster of barns and corrals at the other.

Megan looked around as Ben brought the truck to a stop. "What's this place called?" she asked, fascinated.

Ben came around and opened her door. "I call it home," he said, laughing. "When I'm not living in the trailer at the yacht club, I live here. Come in and meet my mom."

Ben's mother was a petite, dainty woman with dark eyes and dark hair who immediately reminded Megan of Mattie. "I'm glad to meet you," Megan said warmly. "Ben has been such a help with the Tadpoles this summer, and my mom says that she just couldn't get along without Mattie."

Mrs. Holliday smiled and held out her hand. "And we've heard a lot about you," she said. "Ben's impressed with all the things you've accomplished with the children."

149

Ben took Megan's arm. "We'll be back in a little while, Mom," he said. "Come on, Megan, I've got something I want to show you."

He led her to a small corral and whistled. A small sorrel mare trotted over to him and nuzzled his arm gently. "Reno, say hello to Megan. Would you like to ride her?"

"Can I really?" Megan cried delightedly. "But I've never been on a horse before."

Ben shook his head and pretended to frown. "What did I tell you? You've missed out on just about everything that's fun. Now let's saddle up and get going."

Fascinated, Megan watched Ben deftly saddle Reno and his own horse, a high-spirited gray named Sidewinder. In a few minutes they were on their way up a sloping rock-strewn path that led to the top of a hill. For the first few moments in the saddle, Megan felt uncomfortable, but Reno made riding so easy she couldn't help but relax. The trail was beautiful, and when they broke out of the trees and into the open, she gasped in surprise.

"Oh, what a fantastic view!" Below her, the land dropped away steeply to the west, where the sun was setting, a vast expanse of pink, red, and purple. Its reflection painted the trees and hills a warm, rich gold. In the distance a bird sang into the evening, and from the trees behind them, another answered.

Megan sighed. "Ben, it's beautiful up here."

He dismounted and held Reno's reins while she climbed down. "It's my favorite place in the whole world," he said simply. He dropped the reins, and the two horses began to graze in the lush grass.

"Won't they run away?" Megan asked, looking nervously at the horses.

Ben laughed. "No, you don't have to tie a horse up like a sailboat. They know they have to stay put." He took her hand. "Come over here." He led her to a smooth, pink granite outcropping shaped like a giant throne. The rock was flecked with specks of silver mica that glittered in the light of the setting sun.

"Ever since I was a kid I've loved to come here," he said softly, staring out across the gently rolling hills. "But I've never brought anyone up here to share it with me." He turned to Megan, and the soft warmth in his eyes made her catch her breath.

"Thank you," she said simply. "I'm glad you brought me."

Ben put his arms around her and pulled her close. "You know, I haven't kissed you since the evening we went to the rodeo," he whispered into her ear. "And ever since then, I've wondered what it would be like to kiss you again."

Megan raised her hand softly to his face and traced the curve of his lips with her fingers. "Let's find out," she whispered. Ben's mouth met hers. It was the kiss she'd dreamed of all her life, a perfect kiss full of kindness and sweetness and gentle passion. And Megan knew that all her decisions that summer had been right.

Sweet Dreams

Don't miss any of these great new
*Sweet Dreams* romances, on sale soon!

☐ **#61 EXCHANGE OF HEARTS by Janet Quin-Harkin
(On sale April 15, 1984 • 24056-0 • $2.25)**
Fiona's not enjoying her stay as an exchange student in New
Mexico: she misses her boyfriend Simon back in England,
and Taco West, the only boy on the ranch she's staying at,
teases her and treats her like a pesky kid sister. But as
time goes by, Fiona finds that Taco has a tender side too.
Should she stay faithful to the boy she's supposed to love—
or give her heart to the boy she thought she hated?

☐ **#62 JUST LIKE THE MOVIES by Suzanne Rand
(On sale April 15, 1984 • 24057-9 • $2.25)**
Marcy wants to be an actress. So when she gets a walk-on
part in teen idol Lance Newmark's new movie, she puts all
her time and energy into getting more scenes—and more
attention from Lance. Her old friends are quickly becoming
strangers, but it will be worth it when she's a star and has
the boy she's always dreamed about. Won't it?

☐ **THE SWEET DREAMS MAKEUP WORKBOOK:
A GUIDE TO GLOWING SKIN AND A PRETTIER YOU
by Patricia Bozic (On sale April 15, 1984 • 24165-6 • $2.25)**
Beauty's only skin deep . . . but your skin *is* one of the first
things people notice about you. If you want to put your best
face forward, start with THE SWEET DREAMS MAKEUP

WORKBOOK. It's a surefire guide to glowing skin and professional-looking makeup, containing tips on fragrances, lips, lashes, superclean skin, and everything else you need to make the most of your natural beauty.

☐ #63 KISS ME, CREEP by Marian Woodruff (On sale May 15, 1984 • 24150-8 • $2.25)
Every girl at Cabrillo High has a crush on Richie Brennan—except Joy Wilder. She can't stand his smug, conceited attitude or his stupid jokes, especially the romantic ones: he always kids Joy about being in love with her. Then one day she discovers that he's more serious than she thought. Is Richie really a creep—or someone Joy can love?

☐ #64 LOVE IN THE FAST LANE by Rosemary Vernon (On sale May 15, 1984 • 24151-6 • $2.25)
When Alison's boyfriend died in a car race, she didn't think she could ever get over him—until the day she met Billy Kendall. But soon Alison discovers Billy's enthusiasm for motocross, and it seems as if she's doomed to lose the boy she loves . . . again.

Buy these books at your local bookstore or use this handy coupon for ordering: